GW01451613

The Author's Curse

Asha

Published by A Upstone, 2024.

THE AUTHOR'S CURSE

First edition. November 18, 2024.

Copyright © 2024 Asha.

ISBN: 979-8230163176

Written by Asha.

To my dear friend Chitra,

For your unwavering support during one of the most challenging chapters of my life. Your kindness and encouragement gave me strength in a new and unfamiliar world.

Thank you for being my anchor.

'The line between reality and imagination is thinner than we think. Sometimes, our darkest fears are the stories we dare to write.'

Prologue

The first letter came on an ordinary Tuesday morning. Miriam Makena had just finished her morning coffee, the rich scent still lingering in the quiet of her modest Victorian Style home. She stepped out onto the porch, the rainy season air crisp against her skin, and retrieved the usual stack of mail from the box; bills, a magazine, a few flyers for local events. But nestled in the center of the pile was an unmarked, ivory-colored envelope. No return address. No postage mark.

The handwriting was what stopped her, the tight, looping strokes of a hand she didn't recognize. It wasn't a font, it wasn't printed, but something personal, almost intimate. Her name was written across the front, the ink dark and deliberate, as if every letter had been carefully chosen.

Miriam's heart skipped a beat. She had no reason to be nervous. No reason to feel as though something unseen had just passed over her shoulder, a fleeting presence that made her shiver. But as she tore open the envelope, that unexplainable feeling crept in; a sense of foreboding that she couldn't shake. The words inside were crisp, yet the ink seemed to bleed into the paper, an urgency in every letter.

'Dear Miriam,' it began, *'I recently devoured your latest mystery, and let me commend you for your vision. You captured the secrets of Harbel with a depth that most would never dare to*

explore. Few people have the nerve to peek beneath the surface of a place like this, where every street holds a story, and every house harbors whispers of the past.'

Miriam paused, her fingers trembling slightly as she held the letter. The mention of Harbel, her village, the place she had woven into her books for years was not surprising. After all, it was a small village, and its eerie history had inspired many of her works. But this? This felt different. This wasn't just a compliment. This was something else.

The letter continued, its words more chilling with each sentence.

Your description of the old Harbel Hills Rubber wood cabin was unsettling. The way you captured its decay, the sinister feeling that clings to the rotting walls, and the bloodstained floor. I'm glad you didn't shy away from the details. I'd hate to think people like you were too afraid to face the truth about what happened there.'

Miriam's breath caught. The Rubber wood cabin on Harbel Hill. Miriam had heard these tales growing up, even considered using the Rubber wood cabin as inspiration in her novels, but she hadn't yet. And then, the words that made her stomach twist.

'You see, Miriam, I've been watching. I know things about your stories. Things that are more than just fiction. You've touched on truths that are far more dangerous than you realize. And soon, you'll see just how real they can be.'

Miriam dropped the letter, her hands suddenly too cold to hold it any longer. She blinked rapidly, her mind racing. It was a prank, she told herself. A sick joke from someone who had read her books a few too many times. But even as she tried to dismiss it, the words echoed in her mind.

And then, just as quickly, the world outside seemed to freeze.

The wind, once gentle, picked up, rustling the trees with an unnerving sound. A shadow flitted across her porch, brief but unmistakable—someone had been watching her. She turned sharply, but no one was there. No sign of life beyond the quiet village streets.

It wasn't a prank.
This was something darker.
This was no longer fiction.
The game had begun.

Introduction

Miriam Makena had always found solace in words.

A quiet, introspective woman, Miriam had carved out a life in the small village of Harbel, where nothing much ever changed. It was the kind of place where stories bloomed and withered, where the past was a faint echo of forgotten voices and long-lost secrets. As a writer of thrillers, Miriam was used to crafting twisted plots and dark, complex characters; characters who faced the kind of danger and dread that most people only read about in books. Many people thought her life had always been one of calm order. Nobody knew why she moved into this village, but everyone knew about her books, many of the books were in the local library. For many years her life was okay only punctuated by the occasional moment of chaos in her own imagination. Until the letters started.

Handwritten notes that arrived mysteriously in her mailbox or to her door. These days, the mailbox was useless, with occasional bill. Gone were the days when you expected everything to come through the mail. When she opened the mail box, something gnawed at her. The language was familiar, almost too familiar. There were references to things she had written, details she had put into her stories that no one in Harbel should know. At first, she thought it was a sick joke, some fan playing games, a harmless thrill-seeker looking for attention.

But as the letters continued to arrive, their tone darkened, becoming more sinister. Each note seemed to predict the next disaster in Harbel, vandalism, disappearances, and ultimately, a murder that mirrored the shocking finale of one of Miriam's own novels. The boundary between fiction and reality began to blur in ways she couldn't explain, and a growing sense of unease settled in her chest. Someone was watching her. Someone knew her secrets, the ones she had tucked away in the pages of her mind, in her books. But who could know about her in this village?

The pattern was undeniable: every crime, every catastrophe, was somehow tied to her work. And each letter that followed seemed to grow more intimate, more invasive. The writer wasn't just observing her, it like they were reading her life, dissecting it, twisting it into something dark and dangerous.

Soon, Harbel's once peaceful streets turned into a labyrinth of suspicion. Those who had read her books in the plantation started whispering about Miriam's involvement in the crimes. Had she somehow conjured these horrors into being? Was she a part of the terror that was slowly creeping through her quiet village? Or was someone else playing the role of the puppet master, pulling the strings behind the scenes?

With every new letter, Miriam's world shrank. Her once safe and orderly life in Harbel now felt like a maze she couldn't escape. Each day was a race against time, as she desperately tried to uncover the identity of the fan who knew too much, before they could pull her deeper into the twisted story they were writing.

ASHA

But the more she searched for answers, the more elusive they became. The letters were only the beginning. As Miriam's investigation spiraled out of control, she realized that what she was up against was far more terrifying than she ever imagined. Because this wasn't just a game. This was her life. Someone knew her too well, and someone, somewhere, was writing her ending. The question remained, who was this person?

Chapter 1: The First Letter

Miriam Makena opened her mailbox that morning, just as the first chill of the rainy season crept into the sleepy village of Harbel. She expected the usual mundane envelopes, bills, advertisements, maybe a grocery coupon or two but her gaze fell upon an unmarked, ivory-colored envelope that seemed out of place. Nobody really sent her real letters these days, the post office was almost dead these days. People sent emails and messages, not real letters. Checking the letter, her name was written in dark, spindly handwriting that she didn't recognize. There was something about it that made her pause, her fingers hesitant before finally plucking the envelope from the pile.

She stood there in the driveway of her old Victorian Style house, letting the morning breeze drift past as she tore the seal and carefully unfolded the letter. The parchment was heavy, the ink dark and deliberate, almost as if each letter had been carved onto the page.

'Dear Miriam,' it began, *'I recently devoured your latest mystery, and I must commend you for your vision. You captured the secrets of Harbel with a depth that most would never dare to explore. Few people have the nerve to peek beneath the surface of a place like this, where every street holds a story, and every house harbors whispers of the past.'*

ASHA

Miriam frowned, her eyes darting over the words. It was an unusual letter. There was no return address, no signature, and yet the tone was almost intimate, as though the writer had known her for years. Most people referred to her as Ms. Makena but this fan had referred to her as Miriam, she wondered who would call her that apart from her close friends; mind you she didn't have many friends in this village. There were neighbors and acquaintances but not close friends.

'*Your description of the abandoned Rubber wood cabin on Harbel Hills was especially chilling,*' the letter continued. '*The way the wind rattles the loose boards, the dark stain on the floorboards that seems too deep to scrub away, as though even the wood remembers what happened there.*'

A chill snaked down her spine. The abandoned Rubber wood cabin on Harbel Hills had indeed been a local legend—a place wrapped in rumors and half-truths, a structure left to decay on the village's forgotten edge. Years ago, a drifter had wandered into Harbel and made the Rubber wood cabin his home, a man whose face most plantation people barely remembered but whose presence had lodged itself in their memories like a thorn. No one knew his real name; people only remembered him as 'Red,' due to the rough crimson scarf he always wore, faded and frayed like his stories. Red had lived there quietly for months, a shadow in the woods, until one night he vanished without a trace.

But there was something darker that hung around the rubber wood cabin like a specter—whispers of what might have happened that final night. A group of children had stumbled across the rubber wood cabin not long after his disappearance. Drawn by curiosity, they'd dared each other to peek through the cracked windows, to press their faces against the grimy glass. What they saw inside had haunted each of them, details fractured by childhood terror but consistent enough to suggest horror beyond their years.

The children described a single wooden dusty chair with some sort of a rope rotting away in the center of the room, its wooden frame splintered and askew, as though someone had been forcibly restrained. Beneath it, a pool of something dark stained the floorboards, spreading outward like fingers. The smell of iron hung heavy in the air, mingling with the Rubber wood cabin's natural decay. One child claimed to have seen lots of scratch marks gouged into the floorboards around the chair, as if someone had tried desperately to claw their way free. And the walls...they were covered in strange, erratic lines, jagged symbols scrawled in what looked like smeared dirt but might have been something else entirely. They knew it wasn't water or milk for sure and blood for sure is what they were thinking.

The children's discovery sparked an immediate panic. Local authorities were called, mind you there was never a police number that worked in these areas. If you needed a police officer you had either to walk to the thatched looking police station or use (boda boda), the motorbikes that were used to get by quickly. Whoever got to the village's police station at the time found a grizzled man named Officer Jojo who was tasked with the investigation. If asking a few questions is what this part of the world called investigation. But as the days turned into weeks, no evidence turned up, no suspect, no body. Just that chair, the pool of dried blood, and those frantic marks carved into the walls. Office Jojo insisted it was all a misunderstanding, likely the remnants of some desperate hunter's breakdown, but the locals knew better. They said Red had died there, that whatever he'd seen or encountered in that Rubber wood cabin had driven him to madness or death. Police were paid very little money and most of the days they spent their time harassing matatu drivers (the name of small vans that ferried people from one place to the other) and motor bike riders in this village.

And so, the incident like many others faded into the fabric of Harbel's dark history, an unsolved case that locals preferred not to discuss. Every now and then, a brave soul would wander out to the Rubber wood cabin on a dare, only to return with wide eyes and a newfound silence. Over time, people avoided it entirely, the forest reclaiming the path leading up to it, branches casting long shadows across the place like bony fingers. Being a rainforest, the snakes too had found their home.

Miriam who had grown up in the village not very far from here had heard these tales while growing up . She even considered using the Rubber wood cabin as inspiration in her novels, but she hadn't yet. It was a place that, even in fiction, she had shied away from, as if her words might somehow invite whatever evil lingered there back to life. And yet, here it was, captured in vivid detail in the letter she held in her hands; as though her thoughts had been drawn out onto the page by an unseen hand.

'Then there's the Gborie house,' the letter went on. 'The broken window in the upstairs room, your detail was impeccable. It's almost as if you stood outside that night, watching as the shadow moved across the cracked glass.'

The Gborie House. Everyone in Harbel knew it well. It sat at the end of Cotton Lane, just past the church; a once-grand residence, once the pride of old Mr. Gborie, who had inherited it from his grandfather. The Gborie family had once dominated the village, owning most of the buildings, though over time they sold nearly all of them. And though they were well-known, their reputation was less than admirable.

The real scandal came when Laz Gborie returned home one night to find his entire family gone. The villagers had plenty to say, but no one seemed to know what truly happened. The shock was too much for Mr. Gborie, who, some whispered, never recovered. A year later, he died under mysterious circumstances; some said he poisoned himself, others a heart attack. But no one could say for certain.

Since then, the Gborie House had slipped into ruin, abandoned and rotting from the inside out, standing like a dark figure at the edge of the plantation. People murmured that it was cursed, claiming to hear footsteps pacing its creaky floors late at night. Others spoke of a shadowy figure that would appear in the upstairs window or strange noises drifting from the house. It had taken on a life of its own, a ghostly remnant of the past, cloaked in mystery and fear.

Just like the cabin, Miriam hadn't written about it either. In fact, she'd deliberately left the Gborie house out of her books, as though instinctively warding off whatever curse it might hold. And yet here it was, brought to life on this page.

Miriam looked up from the letter, her gaze drifting to her own home; a modest bungalow painted in soft greys with white trim. She'd lived here for years, pouring countless weekends into restoring every inch herself. She had sanded down the old wooden floors, repainted the walls, and installed new fixtures, breathing fresh life into the place. While gardening wasn't her strong suit, she occasionally made an effort to tame the small, unruly patch of greenery out front. The house wasn't grand like the Gborie House had once been, but it was hers, a cozy haven with a view of the quiet street lined by crooked trees, their branches arching toward each other and casting eerie shadows as dusk fell.

Her home sat nestled between her two longtime neighbors: Maggie on one side, a lively waitress at the local diner who always had a smile and a friendly word, and Jackton on the other, a quiet, steady man who'd worked as a driver for one of the local schools for years. Maggie's laughter often echoed through the walls as she shared stories from the diner, while Jackton's calm presence and gentle nods offered a reassuring sense of stability in the neighborhood.

Across the street was Ms. Shah's small bookstore, with its creaky floors and attic packed with dust-covered novels, some even written by Miriam. Ms. Shah's family had come from India decades ago, and though she stocked an assortment of rare herbs, the villagers rarely visited for such things. People whispered that Ms. Shah had been cursed by her family for not marrying as tradition dictated, forced to leave India as an outcast, now living alone in Harbel without any relatives.

The people of Harbel were a tight-knit, insular community; polite yet always keeping a respectful distance, bound by unspoken secrets that lingered beneath the surface, seldom shared with each other or outsiders.

Harbel was a maze of history and mystery, where memories of the past lingered in every corner, intertwining with the present. Every home in the village could name a family member or friend who had been lost during the old war, a tragedy that seemed etched into the very fabric of the village.

A vast rubber plantation stretched beside it, one of the largest in the world and its vastness held secrets known only to the locals. There was the narrow, weathered bridge over Cotton Tree Creek, the overgrown cemetery on the eastern hill where forgotten headstones leaned like weary travelers, and the abandoned Rubber wood cabin on Harbel Hills, a place few dared to enter.

Legends of the past still haunted Harbel, especially the cliff near Cotton Tree, where bodies were rumored to have been thrown during the conflict. It was a spot avoided by all, regarded as haunted, and the villagers raised their children with warnings to steer clear, knowing the weight of the stories that bound them to it.

She turned her gaze back to the letter, reading once more the final line: 'It's as though you were there.'

Miriam's stomach twisted, a creeping unease settling in. She had never written these things, had never put these details to paper, and yet the author of this letter seemed to know exactly what was hidden in her mind, thoughts she had toyed with and abandoned, places she had considered for her stories but never explored. It was as though the writer had pulled these ideas straight from her imagination, fashioning them into reality with chilling precision. It was scary to think of who this person could be.

Miriam folded the letter and slipped it back into the envelope, her hand trembling slightly. She felt watched, as though hidden eyes tracked her every move from behind a curtain or a shadowed corner. Outside, the morning light filtered through the crooked trees along the quiet street, casting soft, golden rays across her neighbors' houses and setting the leaves aglow.

She knew her neighbors well or thought she did. In a town like Harbel, people kept to themselves, but everyone knew everyone else's stories, or thought they did. Maggie's cheerful smile, ever-present during her shifts as a waitress, now seemed almost too bright, as if masking something deeper. Ms. Shah, with her herbs and dusty bookstore, what did she really do when she pulled those heavy curtains shut? And Jackton, where had she seen him before she moved to Harbel? The thought nagged at her, a memory just out of reach.

Everything looked as usual in the soft morning light, but there was an edge to it, a strange sharpness to the ordinary. In the stillness of Harbel's morning, something dark had begun to stir. And as she closed her front door, Miriam couldn't shake the feeling that this was only the beginning.

Chapter 2: A Stranger's Voice

The letter stayed on Miriam's desk all night, a single slip of parchment casting an uncomfortable shadow in her mind. She told herself it was just an overzealous fan, someone too invested in the village's history, or maybe someone trying to spook her for the thrill of it. By morning, she almost believed it. Almost.

Miriam tried to shake the unsettling feeling as she began her morning, the letter tucked into her pocket, its weight somehow heavier than it should have been. She couldn't stop herself from glancing around her quiet street, her eyes drifting to her neighbors' houses as a thought lingered, uninvited, at the edge of her mind: Who could have written it?

As she walked toward the village square, she found herself questioning everyone she passed. Her mind turned first to Mrs. Harriet Juma, the village's self-appointed historian, known for her sharp memory and sharper tongue. Harriet's house was three doors down, an old Victorian Style painted a bright, sickly yellow with lace curtains that seemed to twitch whenever someone walked by. Harriet had often ambled over, brimming with the village gossip, thrilled to update Miriam on the latest happenings; even if 'happenings' amounted to little more than who overwatered their lawn during the scarce water period time, who made the best Jollof rice or who'd finally had their driveway repaved. Was it so hard to imagine Harriet escalating her need to know, her need to be the first with the news, into something more sinister? She knew everyone's secrets; maybe she wanted to stir them into something darker.

But Harriet was anything but subtle. She thrived on attention, the thrill of passing on stories, the satisfaction of a well-spread rumor. Harriet was the last person who'd keep herself hidden behind an anonymous letter. She'd more likely be the one gossiping about the letters in the village. Miriam doubted if she would keep her mouth shut with any news.

Miriam's eyes shifted across the street to Jacob Mendoza, the mysterious Philippine man with graying hair and a long, lined face who worked in his garage at odd hours, hidden behind shelves of tools and endless jars filled with bolts, wires, and screws. 'The Inventor,' as village people called him, was an eccentric fixture in Harbel, living there long before Miriam arrived. With his hunched shoulders and perpetual frown, Jacob barely spoke to anyone, his life seemingly reduced to a private world of half-finished contraptions and greasy blueprints. The idea of Jacob noticing her work enough to recreate it crossed her mind like a faint shadow. Perhaps he had even begun to see himself in one of her characters, his strange and isolated life mirrored on her pages.

But she quickly dismissed the idea; Jacob was too withdrawn, too focused on whatever strange projects consumed his days. He might observe the village from his workshop, but he didn't seem interested in reaching beyond it.

Next, Miriam thought of Patricia Aremu, the mild-mannered librarian whose presence in Harbel was as constant and unassuming as the faint musty scent of the library. Patricia was soft-spoken, the type to nod politely rather than engage in a heated discussion, yet there was a fervor in her gaze, a restrained intensity that always emerged when they talked about books. Patricia had read every one of Miriam's novels, often slipping her notes with book recommendations or articles between the pages of her latest borrow. Had Patricia taken her appreciation a step further, turning from a quiet reader into an anonymous puppet master, orchestrating an eerie game only she understood?

The notion was unsettling. Patricia was friendly, polite, and harmless. Miriam couldn't picture her lurking in the dark, scribbling threatening notes.

She tried to put Patricia out of her mind, but as she crossed the village square, she spotted Tobias, the village carpenter, with his usual morning laugh booming down the street. Tobias was that rare breed of neighbor everyone liked: rough around the edges but effortlessly charming. He always had a grin for Miriam and a habit of making dark jokes about 'borrowing' ideas from her books to commit the 'perfect crime.' She'd laughed along, but those comments always stuck with her just a little too long.

It didn't help that Tobias's main woodworking specialty happened to be coffins; quite the convenient profession for someone who loved a morbid joke. Miriam realized she didn't actually know his last name, and suddenly his friendly grin seemed like a clever cover-up. She couldn't help but wonder if all that laughter was just his way of hiding... something.

But that was just Tobias's sense of humor, she thought, shaking her head. He was mischievous, yes, but not malicious. Still, there was something about the way he looked at her when he joked, something lingering and thoughtful, as if he enjoyed watching her reactions a little too much.

And then her thoughts turned, almost reluctantly, to old Louis Waugh, who had taught nearly everyone in the village at one point or another. Louis spent his days now on his porch at the end of Mason Street, his gaze as sharp as his memory, a walking archive of the village's history. She'd bumped into him at the market last week, where he'd congratulated her on her latest book, his words laced with an eerie undertone. 'You've done us proud, Miriam. Brought our little village to life, every detail so vivid. So true.' She'd felt his gaze linger on her, a knowing look that hinted he understood her work better than most. He was a teacher and good one too and further he had known all the dark corners of Harbel for decades. He could have written this letter, someone like him would know enough about the village's secrets, its shadowy past, to add chilling details.

But it was absurd, she thought. Louis had been respectful to her and a mentor to many children in so many ways. Yet, an edge of doubt remained, a question she couldn't quite brush away.

By the time she made her way back to her house, she'd mentally listed almost everyone in the village who had ever expressed interest in her books, and even those who hadn't. The butcher with his quiet smile, the barber with his unnerving fixation on crime novels, even the corner shop Lebanese guy who sold sweets and date dried fruits.

As Miriam's home came into view, she felt a pang of unease. Usually charming with its arched doorway and cozy front porch, the bungalow now seemed darker, almost ominous under her shifting thoughts. It stood as a reminder that within those walls, she was still alone. The quiet street around her felt oddly watchful; she scanned the trees and the well-trimmed hedges, wondering if someone was lurking, hidden in the shadows, observing her every move.

At forty, Miriam had never been married. Sometimes, she felt a twinge of sadness thinking about Ms. Shah, who had become an outcast in her own family for staying single. Had she been in a culture like that, Miriam might have been seen the same way; unattached and without children at this age. She thought of her routine: the same quiet dinners, the same morning coffee alone, writing, cooking, and doing all the mundane tasks that made up her days. When was the last time she did something genuinely fun? Her life had slipped into a lonely rhythm, but she tried to brush it off.

Then there was Sammy. Her last boyfriend, who had come into her life with a charming smile and just enough mystery to keep her guessing. For a time, he'd seemed perfect. But after a few months, his drinking started to spiral, and the small annoyances turned into big, unavoidable problems. There were those days he'd come home so drunk he'd bang on her door, demanding to be let in like it was his right. The last straw had come when he'd nearly broken her coffee table in a drunken tumble, and with a firm but heavy heart, she'd asked him to leave.

ASHA

Seven years had passed since she'd told him to go, and Sammy had simply vanished from her life. She had no idea where he went, but now, with this growing feeling of someone watching her, she couldn't help but wonder, could it be Sammy? He'd never threatened her outright, but he was just impulsive enough to seek some twisted form of revenge. Maybe that last laugh of his, as he walked out the door, was more than just bravado.

As she stepped inside, she felt the once-comforting walls close in a little. Every familiar nook and cranny, from the worn leather armchair by the window to the shelves stacked with books, seemed a little too quiet, as though her own sanctuary had turned its gaze back on her. She could almost feel a stranger's presence among the shelves, behind the curtains, whispering between the pages of her books.

Was it Harriet? Jacob? Patricia? Tobias? Or maybe Sammy? Or was it someone she'd overlooked entirely, a hidden face in the crowd who saw her even now, saw her in the dark spaces she hadn't noticed, lingering in the shadows, pen in hand, whispering their strange secrets onto the page? As the thought simmered in her mind, her curiosity and fear mingled into an uneasy resolve. She couldn't shake the feeling that someone among these familiar faces held her secrets. One of them was watching her, someone she thought she knew but who lurked in the shadows, shrouded in mystery, hiding behind a mask she'd never noticed. The certainty gnawed at her like a splinter lodged deep in her mind, each passing moment heightening the unease, the suspicion.

Chapter 3: The Second Letter

The following morning, after a restless night piecing together the possible identities of her mysterious correspondent, Miriam told herself it was nothing. A fluke, she thought, over and over, even as her mind wandered back to Harriet, Tobias, Roger; faces of neighbors she barely knew, each with their own peculiar quirks. But surely none of them would go to this length. She was almost convinced it was nothing... when the doorbell rang.

Her heart jolted, and she froze, an icy weight settling in her chest. It's fine, she reassured herself. It's probably just one of the neighbors. Taking a steadying breath, she strode to the door, plastering on an air of indifference. But as she opened it, the familiar sight of another envelope on her doorstep shattered her fragile composure.

It was identical to the first one, no postage stamp, no return address, and this time at her door not her mailbox. Her name again had been written in the same spindly, jagged script. She swallowed hard, the taste of unease creeping up her throat. Her fingers fumbled as she tore the envelope open, bracing herself. This time, the letter was shorter, as if the writer knew she'd already been drawn in, already captivated by their words.

'Miriam,' it began, 'Perhaps yesterday's letter piqued your curiosity. You have a keen eye for detail—something I admire. I thought you might like to know about the burglary on Dedan

Street last night. A pity, really. The Wilsons were such trusting people, always leaving their back door unlocked. But that's Harbel, isn't it? A village lulled by its own complacency.'

Miriam's fingers tightened around the letter as a wave of nausea hit her. She read and reread the words, but they remained a chilling blur. Dedan Street, it was only a few blocks away. She knew the Wilsons, an elderly couple with kind smiles who waved at her each evening as she passed by their garden. Although it was early in the morning, she hadn't heard anything about a break-in. And yet, the letter's tone was certain, as if its author had been there, watching the whole thing unfold.

Her chest tightened, a crawling sensation spreading through her limbs. Fighting to keep her composure, she reached for her phone, quickly dialing the local police station. It was early, and the voice on the other end sounded groggy. Officer Jerome, a young recruit, listened to her stammered inquiry before confirming, almost sleepily, that there had indeed been a burglary at the Wilsons' home last night.

'No one was hurt,' he said, though his voice sounded uncertain, 'but they were pretty shaken up. Just some jewelery and some cash missing. The intruder slipped in quietly. No trace was left behind, other than a broken vase and some muddy footprints.' He was quick to add not worry Ms. we will look further into it.

Miriam's pulse thundered as she thanked Officer Jerome and ended the call, her mind spinning, how did the writer know about the break in, were they there, did there? break the house? The house felt unbearably silent, each creak in the floor, each ticking of the clock amplified, until the quiet itself seemed to press down on her. Miriam always liked coffee in the morning and it helped her start her writing by clearing her mind but this morning coffee couldn't help.

Why had the stranger chosen her? She stared at the letter, her fingers trembling as she gripped it tightly. How could this person know about the burglary this early morning, write the letter and bring the letter to my door? Her thoughts raced back to last night, to the faces of her neighbors she'd tried to dismiss. But now they resurfaced, their idle smiles and friendly nods twisted in her mind. Who could it be? Who was this 'fan' who seemed to know more than they should?

A prickling sensation crept over her skin, and instinctively, Miriam glanced toward the window, half-expecting to meet a pair of eyes watching her from the shadows. But outside, the street lay desolate. Parked cars lined the curb, their wet surfaces gleaming under the intermittent glow of flickering street lights, which cast restless shadows across the pavement. Rain drizzled down in a thin, relentless sheet, and the whole day seemed weighed down by a peculiar heaviness, as though something unseen lurked in the damp air.

She drifted through the motions of the morning, but everything felt off, hollow. Her usual rituals failed her; the coffee tasted metallic, bitter on her tongue, and even the simple task of making toast felt like an unbearable effort. She thought of trying to meditate, something she'd seen recommended on a morning talk show, but her mind refused to settle. The worry gnawed at her, its presence as constant as the rain outside, pressing down on her thoughts, tightening her chest.

It was as though the letter had cast a dark spell over everything, seeping into her home, her mind, turning even the familiar into something unsettling. She could feel it there, just within her grip, the answers and the horrors they promised, waiting to seep into her life and pull it apart piece by piece.

The hours crawled by, each second dragging her deeper into a spiral of anxiety, and with every passing moment, Miriam's mind filled with the gnawing dread that another letter might arrive; another message from her anonymous tormentor. By afternoon, her once-cozy home felt like a prison, its walls pressing in, trapping her in a relentless loop of fear. She paced from room to room, trying to shake the feeling, but every creak of the floorboards, every flicker of a shadow seemed amplified, heightening her nerves and setting her pulse racing.

THE VERY AIR FELT THICK, clinging to her skin, almost suffocating, as if her unseen watcher were lurking somewhere nearby, close enough to touch, breathing down her neck. She tried to shake the feeling, to focus, to rationalize the situation somehow. Desperately, she took out a notepad and wrote down every name she could think of from Harbel, the old fishmongers at the market, the vegetable sellers, even passing acquaintances she barely knew. She listed, analyzed, and cross-examined each name, struggling to imagine why any of them might be behind the letters.

But the exercise felt hopeless, pointless, her suspicion flaring and fading with each name. No one quite fit, and nothing gave her a shred of relief. Was she slipping into paranoia? Had this mystery already unraveled her mind? She sank into a chair, hands trembling, her heart racing faster as the thought surfaced, unbidden: What if this was all in her head? But no, she wasn't imagining the letters, was she? The paper, the words, the messages, the chilling familiarity in every line.

She spent the rest of the day in a haze, thoughts racing, replaying every word of the letter, every odd smile she'd received in passing, every neighbor's face she'd ever seen on the street. She could no longer tell where her suspicions ended and her paranoia began. Each creak of the house, each whisper of wind outside, felt sinister, as if the walls themselves were closing in.

Finally, as the last remnants of daylight seeped away, she slumped into her armchair, forcing herself to open her favorite book, hoping the familiar words would distract her from the feeling that something terrible was coming. But each line only brought her back to the letters, to the stranger's voice that seemed to float around her, lingering in every corner.

As the shadows lengthened, she told herself it was nothing. Just a fluke, she thought, forcing her thoughts away from the letter. She was almost convincing herself when, in the encroaching darkness, she heard a faint sound at the door. The sound even though very faint sliced through the silence, shattering the fragile illusion of safety she'd been clinging to. Her heart hammered as she rose slowly, each step toward the door feeling like a descent into some dark, uncharted territory.

She opened the door, and there it was... a third letter, lying on the mat like a shadow cast across her day. It looked innocent enough, but its very weight seemed to promise darker revelations. Miriam hesitated, a surge of resistance flaring within her. A quiet urge to leave it untouched, to ignore whatever fresh horrors awaited inside. But the compulsion was too strong.

As she reached down, dread crept up her spine, a chill certainty settling deep in her chest. This letter, like the others, was bound to unravel the fragile threads of her life. With the envelope clutched tightly in her hand. In her grip, it felt both heavy and electric, as if it held both the answers she feared and the terrors she wished to bury.

Chapter 4: The Third Letter

Miriam locked the door with a mechanical click, the sound echoing hollowly in the otherwise silent house. It was a reflex, an action she performed without thinking, even though she knew the truth deep down. It wouldn't stop them. The feeling of being watched had taken root in her chest, an ever-tightening knot that no lock or bolt could undo. There was no safe space left.

She stood in the dim hallway, fingers gripping the envelope tightly, as if its contents could somehow anchor her. A heavy sense of foreboding hung in the air, thick and suffocating, transforming her once-comforting home into a silent, looming mausoleum. The stillness pressed in, each second stretching into an endless, breathless eternity. Her gaze drifted to the portrait she had hung on the wall only days before, a time when life had seemed good, steady. She was a successful author, content with her life and her home, dreaming of distant shores and new horizons. In the back of her mind, she'd always known that this village might not be enough. One day, she imagined, she would move to the coast, settling near the ocean, where she could write her books as waves crashed against the shore, and the sand beneath her feet sparked fresh inspiration along the endless coastline.

She snapped out of her reverie of the distant coastline, her fingers trembling as she turned the envelope over, scrutinizing it as if it concealed some dark, forbidden truth. The paper felt rough, almost brittle under her touch, like it had been weathered by years of secrets; its edges frayed, as though it had lingered in the shadows, gathering whispers and hidden intentions. She sensed a strange, ominous deliberateness this time, an eerie finality that tightened around her chest like a vice.

Her breath quickened, and a shiver crept up her spine, prickling her skin with a cold certainty that this was more than a mere letter. This was a summons, a call from some shadowy past she had never intended to revisit. The envelope felt heavier now, weighted by secrets she feared to unravel. Was it a warning? A threat? Or something worse, something with the power to pull her into a darkness she couldn't escape?

As she stared at it, the hallway grew dimmer, the shadows around her thickening, as though the house itself was conspiring to keep her rooted in place, ensnared in its silent menace. She tried to breathe, but the air felt stale, thin, as if every ounce of oxygen had been drained. The dreams of exotic shores and the comfort of her home faded, leaving only an unshakable sense of dread that clung to her like a cold, damp fog.

In that moment, she knew: whatever waited inside the envelope was not just a message. It was a doorway, an invitation into something darker and more dangerous than she had ever known.

THE AUTHOR'S CURSE

With a quiet, almost reverent motion, she tore open the flap. The letter slid free, and she unfolded it with slow, deliberate care. Each movement felt measured, as though the contents of the letter were so potent, so dangerous, that any misstep might unleash something worse than she was prepared for.

'Miriam,' the letter began. The familiar greeting, yes, but there was no warmth in it this time. No trace of the playful intrigue that had characterized the first two letters. This time, the words felt colder, sharper and more like a knife's edge than an invitation. They seemed to carve themselves into the paper, leaving a permanent mark that dug into her consciousness.

'I see you've been thinking about me,' the letter continued. 'It's only natural. You're a writer, after all. It must be maddening to have a story unraveling at your doorstep, one you didn't write, one you can't control. I can't blame you for feeling trapped. I would, too. The walls must feel like they're closing in.'

Miriam's breath hitched, her pulse quickening as she read the words. The writing was so eerily precise, so unsettling in its observation of her life. They began to feel as if it were spoken directly into her ear. Each sentence twisted into her thoughts, worming its way into her mind until she could no longer tell where the letter ended and her own thoughts began.

'But don't worry, Miriam. I'll make sure you have all the details you need. After all, I've been keeping my eye on you for a long time, just like I've been keeping my eye on others.'

Miriam's heart thundered against her ribcage, each beat louder than the last as the words burrowed deep, chilling her to the bone. Her mind began to replay moments she had once dismissed, now tainted by this poisonous revelation. She could almost hear a whisper threading through the corners of her mind, a voice she hadn't noticed before, lurking in the shadows, brushing against her thoughts.

A sick realization crept over her: someone had been watching her. Watching her every movement, every quiet breath, weaving themselves into her life, her most intimate moments. How long had this shadow existed, lingering just beyond her awareness? Her skin crawled as she thought of it, a wave of betrayal washing over her, blending with a fear so raw it carved an emptiness inside her.

The security she had wrapped around herself all these years shattered, leaving her exposed and vulnerable. What she thought was peace had been a lie, a fragile illusion that had masked this unseen presence. Fury roared within her, mingling with hurt, disgust, and a bone-deep invasion that she couldn't name. Her trust, her privacy, all stolen. All she could feel now was a searing rage that clawed its way to the surface, twisting with emotions she hadn't known existed, and a gnawing question: How much of herself had been laid bare, and to whom?

The letter continued, pulling her deeper into the web.

'You know about the Gborie House? Any recall of similar incidents? That's where I'm from. It's a shame really, what happened there. A family, so trusting, so eager to believe in the safety of their home. But someone, someone they never saw coming, taught them a lesson.'

Miriam's hand flew to her mouth, the blood draining from her face. The words blurred in front of her eyes, but she couldn't stop reading, couldn't tear her gaze away from the page. The Gborie House. The abandoned house on the outskirts of Harbel. Left to rot, an eyesore on the village's otherwise sleepy streets. She knew the stories, of course. Everyone did. But hearing it in writing, hearing it come from the pen of the person who had invaded her life, made it real in a way that chilled her to the core.

The letter continued, as if it knew the exact moment her mind had frozen. It felt like it was toying with her, pulling her into the past, forcing her to relive the dark history of the village she thought she knew.

'The break-ins started small, harmless even,' it said. 'Little things, coins missing from the jar, a book out of place. But then one night, there was no stopping it. The father came home to find his family... gone.'

A cold wave of nausea swept over Miriam. Gone. The word seemed to hang in the air, an accusation. She had heard the rumors about the family, Gborie who everyone had something strange to say about him, strange disappearances, deaths. But no one had ever spoken about it with such chilling finality. She swallowed hard, her throat dry, as she clutched the letter tighter, the paper digging into her fingers as if it could anchor her to reality.

The letter seemed to grow heavier with each word, as though its very weight was pressing down on her, closing in on her thoughts, her breath, her sanity. The writer knew things about the Gborie house that only someone who had been there or who had watched, could know.

'It wasn't the first death in Harbel, but it was the most memorable,' the letter continued, each line carrying a weight she could barely bear. 'The village has a way of forgetting, of moving on. But I remember. And soon, so will you.'

Miriam's head spun. The connection between the break-in at the Wilsons' house, the Gborie House, the strange letters, it was too much. Her mind raced, trying to piece it all together, but the pieces didn't fit. They couldn't. There was no way this could be real.

And yet, every word of the letter carried a ring of truth, an undeniable certainty that shook her to her core. Whoever was behind this knew everything! Every detail of her life, every small, insignificant thing she had ever done. She felt the invisible eyes of the writer on her, felt their gaze seeping through the cracks of her defenses, like cold fingers brushing against her skin.

Her stomach churned as the weight of it all settled in her chest. The house didn't feel safe; she was no longer in a safe place. The windows she had once relied on for light and air now felt like openings into something unknown, something sinister. The walls, which had always provided shelter, now seemed fragile, almost paper-thin, as though they could collapse at any moment under the weight of what was coming.

Miriam glanced toward the window, half-expecting to see the dark outline of a figure standing just outside, watching her with cold, unblinking eyes. But the street was empty, the same as it had always been. No one was there. No one ever was.

But that was the point, wasn't it? They didn't need to be there. They were already inside her head, inside her thoughts, playing their twisted game. They knew things no one else could.

THE AUTHOR'S CURSE

Her hand trembled as she set the letter down on the table, the paper crackling under her fingertips. Her thoughts spiraled, racing in every direction, but they always came back to the same question: Who was this person?

And more importantly, Why her?

She put the letter in her bag, her fingers still trembling from its cold, deliberate touch. The air in her house felt thick with a kind of suffocating tension that had only deepened since the letter arrived. She couldn't stay here, trapped inside her own walls, waiting for something she couldn't see. No, she needed to do something! Anything, to break the cycle of fear.

With a deep breath, Miriam stood and pulled her jacket over her shoulders. The house had become a prison, and she refused to sit in it any longer. She needed to leave, to move, to gather some semblance of control. Her mind buzzed with the need to piece things together, to make sense of the chaos, and the only way she could do that was by talking to people, observing people too, by looking for answers in the faces of the village folk who seemed to live their ordinary lives while she was crumpling.

She grabbed her bag and left through the front door, the cool morning air biting her skin as she stepped out onto the quiet street. The village of Harbel was still sleeping, or at least it seemed that way. The streets were calm, the usual hum of life barely stirring. But Miriam didn't mind the silence. It gave her space to think, to plan.

She moved with purpose, walking down familiar streets, her eyes scanning the faces of passersby, trying to detect any sign of recognition, any hint that she might know the person behind the letters. The world felt different now, as if everything had shifted and she was the only one who noticed. Each person she saw, each face she passed, was a potential clue. Could it be the grocer, the librarian, the milkman? She couldn't be sure, but she had to start somewhere.

She spent the day in the village square, at the coffee shop, and in the market, speaking small talks to anyone to find out who might know something or anything that could explain the letters. Each interaction felt forced, like a performance. Her nerves were taut, her senses on high alert, but nothing unusual happened. People greeted her with friendly smiles and small talk, their faces no more familiar than they had been the day before. Miriam couldn't shake the feeling that she was being watched, but it was impossible to tell from where. The letters had poisoned her view of Harbel, turning every corner, every face, into a potential threat.

She'd scanned every face, asked every question, but no answers had come. She couldn't reveal to these people about the letters she was receiving. She feared people would start talking about her if they weren't already doing it. It was as though the person behind the letters was a ghost, untouchable, their presence felt but never seen. The frustration gnawed at her, but she refused to go back to the safety of her home without at least trying to uncover something. She couldn't be trapped by fear forever. However, by the time the sun began to set, Miriam was exhausted, both physically and mentally. She hadn't found anything concrete, no clear suspects.

When she finally returned home, the house was dark, the silence greeting her like an old friend. She stepped inside, her heart still racing from the day's events, and closed the door behind her. The familiar comfort of her home felt distant now, like a shell, empty and hollow.

But something was different.

On the kitchen counter, just inside the door, lay a new envelope. The fourth letter.

Her pulse quickened as she approached it, her mind reeling. She had been gone long, so it was possible that anyone could have slipped in and stayed in her home all day. The letter was there, waiting for her as though it had always been. She could feel her breath catch in her throat, the weight of the letter almost unbearable in her hands. It was thinner than the last one, the paper crisp and cold, its very presence an accusation.

With a steady hand, she picked it up, already knowing what it would say. She couldn't stop herself now. She had to open it.

The flap tore easily this time, and the letter slid out in a smooth motion, as though it had been prepared for her return. She unfolded it, her hands steady now, as the words began to imprint themselves on her mind.

'Did you enjoy your little excursion today, Miriam?' it read. 'I see you've been looking for answers, trying to outsmart me, trying to find the one thing that would make sense of all this. But here's the truth: you can't. Not yet. Not until you're ready to face what's been staring at you all along.'

A cold chill raced down her spine. She had barely stepped inside her own house, and already the letter seemed to mock her efforts, to twist them into something more sinister. The writer had known she would go out. Had known she would try to find them.

'Look closer, Miriam. The answers are always right in front of you. And when you finally realize it, when you understand who I am, it will be too late.'

The words burned into her consciousness. She stared at the letter, her mind racing, trying to make sense of the cryptic message, trying to make the connections that seemed just out of her reach.

But it was no use. There was no clarity. No escape. The walls of her home, her sanctuary, had once again become a cage. How do you fight a ghost, she wondered?

The fourth letter was another warning, and Miriam realized—too late—that this time, the game was no longer just about finding the truth. It was about surviving long enough to discover it.

And that, more than anything, terrified her.

Chapter 5: The Repercussions

The morning fog clung to the streets like a heavy blanket, a suffocating grayness that seemed to seep into everything it touched. The village of Harbel, usually quaint and peaceful, was now a place where every whisper of wind, every creak of the old wooden buildings, felt like an ominous prelude. Miriam walked down the path from her house, her footsteps muffled by the damp earth, each step feeling like an echo in the empty streets. It was as though the village had collectively held its breath, waiting for something else to happen.

The world outside her door had shifted in a way that felt too deliberate, too calculated. There was no denying it anymore. The letters were part of something bigger, something darker than she could have ever imagined. The fourth letter still burned in her mind. Its words had etched themselves into her consciousness, twisting her thoughts into knots, making her question everything. *Look closer, Miriam. The answers are always right in front of you.* The warning echoed like a drumbeat, louder with each passing moment.

She passed by the bakery, the scent of freshly baked bread, once so comforting, now felt strangely hollow. The baker, Mrs. Harris, gave Miriam a knowing smile, but it was a smile that didn't reach her eyes, as though she, too, was aware of the unsettling change that had overtaken the village. As Miriam continued down the street, she noticed more than a few familiar faces, people she had seen a hundred times before now appeared different. The lines on their faces seemed deeper, their gazes distant, as if the weight of unspoken secrets hung over them.

The usual bustle of the village square was stilled, as though someone had reached down and pressed a mute button on the day. The lively market chatter was gone, replaced by an unsettling hush that settled thickly over the square. Only the occasional rustle of leaves stirred the air, and even that seemed to shiver with tension. The hawkers, usually shouting to sell their bananas, peanuts, and fish stood silently, their shoulders drooping, eyes lowered. It was as if an unseen weight had pressed down upon them, a force too strong to resist. Was it the heavy, humid air clinging to the village, the overcast sky threatening rain, or was it all in her mind?

Miriam scanned the scene, noticing the strange shift in everyone's movements. The people moved with an eerie slowness, almost like specters gliding through the mist, their eyes flickering nervously to shadows and alleyways. It was as though the village had slipped into a strange, muted dimension where time itself felt warped, where everyone seemed to be holding their breath, waiting for something or someone to emerge. She wondered if she was the only one sensing this strange heaviness, or if this quiet unease had gripped the village itself, changing it into something almost unrecognizable.

It didn't take long for Miriam to hear the first rumors. They started in hushed tones as she walked past groups of people, mothers exchanging worried glances, elderly men muttering in the corner of the local pub, all with the same unease in their voices. At first, it was vandalism. Graffiti scrawled across the walls of the old church, mocking symbols that no one seemed to understand but everyone feared. Next, it was the missing pets; dogs, cats, even a rabbit. Pets that had vanished in the night, without a trace, leaving only the hollow echo of their absence.

And then, the most shocking of all, the death of Gerald Turner, the beloved local teacher. His death wasn't just a tragedy, it was a mystery. Found lying in the middle of the street, no signs of struggle, no obvious cause. Just an empty, lifeless shell of a man who had been one of the village's most cherished residents.

Miriam couldn't escape the feeling that all of it, the vandalism, the missing pets, the death of Gerald was somehow tied to the events unfolding around her. Every time she saw a missing pet poster or heard another rumor about the strange occurrences in the village, a nagging thought twisted at her insides. This feels familiar. It was in the air, in the way the village people now spoke, in the silence that followed her every step.

It felt like a chapter from one of her own books, one she hadn't yet written. The same unease that her characters felt in the midst of chaos now clawed at her from the inside out. She was the protagonist now, wasn't she? Living through a nightmare she couldn't control. But the question was who was the villain? And more importantly, what was the endgame?

Later that afternoon, Miriam sat at her desk, the dim light of her study casting long shadows across the room. The bookshelves around her, once filled with stories of adventure, mystery, and comfort, now seemed oppressive, like the walls of her own private jail. She could feel the weight of the books pressing down on her, their stories now becoming tangled in the strange events happening around her. Her fingers hovered over the pages of one of her novels, and for a moment, she wondered if she had somehow written the future into existence.

But no, it wasn't just that. The stories she had written had always been works of fiction. But these events, the ones happening now, felt too real. Too personal.

Her mind spun back to the fourth letter. *Look closer.*

The words haunted her, and yet, she couldn't bring herself to understand what they meant. The village was in the grip of something dark, something far more sinister than the mundane crimes she had first chalked them up to. It was as if the village itself was becoming the backdrop of a tragic tale, a narrative she was now trapped in.

She tried to distract herself, turning her attention to the shelves filled with her books, as though they might offer some sort of solace. But as she scanned the spines, something caught her eye, one book, a collection of short stories she had written years ago, stood out. The stories inside were filled with dark themes of loss, isolation, and betrayal, tales of people unraveling in their own despair. One story in particular; a story about a small village plagued by a string of inexplicable events came rushing back to her memory. It was an old draft, one she had never finished, but as she flipped through the pages, her breath caught.

THE AUTHOR'S CURSE

The events she had written about in the story mirrored what was happening in Harbel. The missing pets. The vandalism. The mysterious death. And the most chilling part? The protagonist in the story had felt exactly the way she did now, isolated, paranoid, and hunted by something unseen.

Her hands shook as she dropped the book, the cold realization settling over her like a shroud. It was as if Harbel's fate had been written long before it all began. She hadn't created this chaos, but somehow, it was as if the words she had penned all those years ago had come to life, and now the consequences were spilling out into her world.

The connection was undeniable, and as the sun dipped below the horizon, casting long shadows across her study, Miriam realized that the only way out of this nightmare was to face it head-on. She had to look closer, as the letter had said. She had to look into the heart of this twisted tale before it consumed her, before the boundaries between her stories and reality blurred beyond recognition.

The air in the room felt colder now, and Miriam wrapped her arms around herself as the weight of what she had uncovered pressed down on her chest. She couldn't ignore the truth any longer. Whatever was happening in Harbel was not just happening by chance. It was a story with a beginning, a middle, and an end and Miriam was now its unwilling lead character.

But who, or what, was the author?

Miriam often found herself sifting through the foggy fragments of her childhood, piecing together memories that felt both painfully vivid and agonizingly distant. She remembered having a younger brother, a quiet boy who had once clung to her side in their shared moments of fleeting comfort. But they had drifted apart, their bond severed by forces far beyond their understanding.

Her father loomed largest in those fragmented memories, a shadowy figure whose presence filled every room with tension. Miriam feared him deeply. His temper, unpredictable and sharp, was like a thunderstorm, silent one moment, explosive the next. His harsh words cut deep, and the heavy weight of his disapproval hung over her like a suffocating shroud. She learned early to stay quiet, to avoid his gaze, and to make herself small when he was near.

When she was thirteen, her life splintered irreparably. Her parents had left, taking her little brother with them, a boy of just seven, clutching a worn teddy bear in his tiny hands as they disappeared down the driveway. They moved to another town, another life, leaving Miriam behind. The reasons were never clear, but the sting of abandonment was sharp and raw. Her father's stern, cold face offered no explanations, only a silent confirmation that she was no longer part of their plans.

Left to care for her aging grandmother, Miriam quickly found herself shouldering responsibilities far beyond her years. The house, once a place of family, felt like a tomb, echoing with emptiness and filled only with her grandmother's quiet shuffles and tired sighs. Miriam often felt like the caretaker rather than the child.

And yet, through it all, a gnawing guilt clung to her. Though no one had ever said it aloud, she couldn't shake the feeling that she had done something wrong, that somehow, she was to blame for the rift that tore her family apart. It was a weight she carried in silence, her father's shadow still looming over her even in his absence.

When her grandmother passed away shortly after, it felt like the final blow. Miriam was alone, with no one left to anchor her. What followed was a hazy stretch of time that she couldn't quite piece together. She couldn't remember the day she was placed in foster care or understand why she hadn't gone to live with her parents. That chapter of her life was blank, as if her mind had decided to close and lock the doors on those painful memories. She hadn't tried to force them open; instead, she let them fade, a past she no longer wished to carry.

By the time she left for college, Miriam knew one thing: she had no desire to revisit the fragments of her past. Writing became her escape, her solace. She'd always been drawn to the power of words; even as a child, she could be found with a pen and a notebook, scribbling the thoughts and fears she couldn't speak aloud. The things she couldn't verbalize took shape on paper, where they felt safer and less tangled. In her notebooks, she created stories where her pain couldn't reach her, filling the pages with worlds that were hers alone. Writing wasn't just a passion; it was her way of finding control over the things she'd lost, a shield against the questions she'd never answered.

Chapter 6: Lines of Fiction

The air in Harbel had shifted. It was no longer just a village, no, it had become a place where reality itself seemed to stretch, contort, and unravel. The weight of it pressed against Miriam's chest like a hand she couldn't shake, a constant, suffocating reminder that whatever was happening here, it was bigger than her. Bigger than anything she could have imagined.

The morning after the fourth letter arrived, Miriam found herself standing at the edge of the village square, staring at the familiar streets that once gave her comfort. Now, they were nothing more than a maze of forgotten memories and lingering dread. She had promised herself she wouldn't let fear dictate her life, but it was hard to hold onto that resolve when every step felt like an intrusion into a world she no longer understood.

She had spent hours last night pacing, rereading the letter again and again, as if the words could somehow offer her clarity. But all they gave her was a sense of growing panic. Look closer, the letter had said. But how could she? How could she possibly see what was hidden beneath the surface when the very ground she walked on felt as if it might crumble away at any moment?

Her mind was a whirlwind, a storm of confusion, fear, and a strange kind of sick curiosity. She had to understand what was happening, she needed answers, no matter the cost. But where could she even begin? The crimes in the village had escalated from petty vandalism to missing pets and, most disturbingly, a murder. The death of Gerald Turner had shattered something in the community. The older generation mourned, but the younger ones whispered about the inexplicable violence, the strange way the village seemed to be morphing into something unrecognizable.

Miriam was no detective, but she had always prided herself on noticing things; patterns, details that others might miss. Maybe that's what the writer saw in her, the writer who was pulling her into this twisted game. But as she stood there, staring out at the gray, damp street, she realized something. This wasn't just a mystery. It wasn't a game. It was real, and it was coming for her.

I'm already too deep, she thought bitterly, a cold dread creeping up her spine. The investigation, the letters, the crimes, everything was connected. She was no longer just a passive observer, detached from the world around her. No, she was a part of this story. The writer had made sure of that. And no matter how much she tried to turn away, the pull of it was too strong.

Her phone buzzed in her pocket, breaking her from her thoughts. She pulled it out, her hands trembling as she glanced at the screen. A message from the same unknown number.

ASHA

The vandalism continues, Miriam. Just wait—there will be more. Watch closely. You're already seeing the beginning, but the end is where things get interesting. How long before you lose your own grip on reality? She knew it was the same writer who had sent the letters but how did he/she get her number?

The message was brief, yet its words reverberated through Miriam's very bones. It felt like a prophecy, as if the writer held an intimate, unnatural knowledge that no one should have. Her breath hitched, a wave of nausea washing over her as a horrifying thought crept in—what if this wasn't some stranger, but someone closer? A family member, perhaps... her mother? Or maybe her brother, no longer the little boy she remembered. Could everything she had written, every step she had taken in life, have somehow drawn her here, to this unsettling moment?

Miriam knew she couldn't sit idly by, letting the fate of the village hang by a thread. She felt the urgency rising within her, the need to act. She knew where to start—with her mother. It had been years, but she remembered the address, just an hour's drive from the village. Her brother lived somewhere nearby, though she hadn't seen either of them in over thirty years. The thought of confronting her past filled her with a mixture of dread and resolve. Whatever the truth was, it was time to uncover it.

As Miriam pulled up to the small house, a strange thrill of anticipation and dread coursed through her. She had never been here before, yet she knew every detail from years of research. It felt surreal to be so close to the family she had only imagined for decades. Taking a steadying breath, she climbed the steps and was about to knock when the door creaked open, and a man stood in the doorway, arms crossed, his expression cold. She blinked, taking in the hard lines of his face, the set of his jaw.

It took a second to register, but this was Andrew; her little brother, though the boy she remembered was nowhere to be seen. He was tall, with lines of age etched into his face. He squinted, studying her, his expression flickering with something between curiosity and irritation.

'Yes?' he asked, his tone guarded.

'Andrew... It's me,' she said, feeling strangely small under his gaze. 'It's Miriam.'

He blinked, taken aback, his eyes widening slightly before narrowing in suspicion. 'Miriam?' he echoed, as if testing the name, turning it over in his mind.

A strained silence hung between them, thick with unspoken questions. Miriam could see the flicker of recognition dawning in his eyes, a shock he was trying to conceal. He gave her a slow once-over, his gaze lingering on her face, as if matching it with something in his memory.

'So you're her,' he said finally, the faintest hint of a smirk playing on his lips. 'The famous writer.' He leaned against the doorframe, crossing his arms as he looked her over. 'I've seen your picture in your books. Even read one or two.'

She swallowed, feeling the weight of his words, his voice lined with something sharper than she had expected. 'I came because... I wanted to talk to mum,' she said, her voice faltering.

Andrew's face darkened, his lips pressing into a thin line. 'Of course, you didn't,' he replied, his tone flat, each word like a stone cast into a well. 'She passed away. Cancer. She held on as long as she could, but you weren't around to see it.' A pang of guilt cut through her, but she steadied herself, meeting his gaze. 'I didn't know, Andrew. I wish I had—'

He held up a hand, cutting her off. 'Don't. I've heard enough about wishes and regrets to last a lifetime. You made your choices,' he said, an unreadable expression flickering across his face. 'Some people get to walk away and leave everything behind.'

The bitterness in his voice felt pointed, though Miriam couldn't tell if it was directed at her or something deeper. 'Andrew... I just thought, maybe I could... find some answers. Understand what I missed.' She could hear the desperation in her own voice, though she tried to hide it.

He laughed, a short, humorless sound. 'Answers?' he repeated, shaking his head. 'There's no answer you'll find that'll fix things, Miriam. Some things just stay buried.' His eyes met hers, and for a brief moment, she saw a flash of something unsettling. 'But I suppose you know all about keeping things buried, don't you?'

A chill ran down her spine. His words were ambiguous, laced with a dark edge, and yet they sounded disturbingly familiar, the language of the letters. The hairs on the back of her neck prickled. Did he know about them? Or was this just another piece of their shared, fractured history he was keeping from her? He looked past her, shrugging as if dismissing her entirely. 'Look, I'm not here to relive the past with you, Miriam. You made it this far without us. Why change that now?'

THE AUTHOR'S CURSE

Miriam tried to hold his gaze, but it felt as if her world was shifting, twisting. She had come looking for answers, but it felt like she was plunging into a maze of suspicion and mistrust. She hadn't seen her family in years, and now, even they felt like strangers or worse, suspects. There was nothing else to say, Miriam got into her car and drove back to Harbel.

Chapter 7: Filed in Silence

With a quiet resolve, she left the mum's house and drove straight to the police station in her village. The small building, with its peeling paint and flickering light, seemed out of place in a village like this, as if it had forgotten its purpose. The officers inside were sluggish, disinterested in the crimes that had rocked their community. They hadn't connected the dots, not in the way she had. But Miriam knew she had to try. Maybe she was grasping at straws, but there was something about the way things were unfolding, something about the eerie rhythm of the events that felt far too orchestrated to be random.

As she approached the door, she hesitated for a moment, the weight of the past few days pressing down on her. There was a strange, unsettling feeling that had followed her everywhere she went, like eyes on her back, like she was being watched from every corner. It made her skin crawl. Her fingers trembled as she reached for the handle, pushing the door open with a soft creak.

The air inside was thick with the smell of stale coffee and cigarette smoke. A few officers sat at their desks, the low hum of conversations barely rising above the sound of a flickering ceiling fan. Miriam approached the front desk, where Officer Joshua, a man with a tired face and a permanent scowl, sat reading through a stack of paperwork.

'Officer Joshua, I need to speak with you,' Miriam said, her voice steady but strained. He looked up at her, an eyebrow raised in silent judgment.

'What about?'

'It's about the crimes. The things happening in the village... I think they're connected,' Miriam said, her voice growing more desperate. 'I need to know more about the cases, the vandalism, the missing pets, Gerald Turner's death.'

Joshua sighed and leaned back in his chair, rubbing his temples as if her words were an unwanted interruption. 'Lady, you're not the first to come in here with these theories. People are upset, sure, but what you're talking about is just coincidence. There's no connection.'

'I don't think it's a coincidence,' Miriam insisted, her voice rising. 'I think someone's behind it all. And I think it's someone who's been watching us. Someone who knows us.'

Joshua's gaze hardened, his expression skeptical. 'So what are you saying? You think this is some kind of game? Some mystery writer's fantasy?' Do you have anything to do with the crimes? Maybe we can start from there.

Miriam's stomach twisted. 'I... I don't know who is doing the crimes. But..... She stopped herself. She couldn't bring up the letters, not yet. It would be too much. They would laugh her out of the room or accuse her of committing the crimes or knowing who was committing them. 'But I think it's bigger than all of us, 'she said.

Joshua didn't say anything for a long moment, his eyes narrowing as if calculating whether she was worth his time. 'If you want to help, Miriam, start by staying out of it. This village's already got enough problems.'

ASHA

With that, he turned back to his paperwork, dismissing her with a cold indifference. She stood there for a moment, staring at the back of his head, feeling the weight of her frustration settle heavily in her chest. The police weren't going to help her. She would have to face this on her own, like she had always done.

As she left the station, a sudden chill gripped her, the village square now bathed in an eerie twilight glow. The streets felt empty, even though they were crowded with people, all of them too consumed by their own fears to notice the woman standing in the middle of it all; lost, desperate, and drowning in secrets.

Her phone buzzed again.

The missing cat, Miriam. You think it's just a pet, don't you? You think it's just another innocent victim. But pay attention, its collar was left behind. Look at the collar closely. I'm waiting for you to see it.

Miriam's pulse quickened as she glanced down at the message, her hands shaking. She could feel it now, the slow creep of panic building in her chest. The writer's words were no longer just warnings. They were truths. And they were slowly suffocating her.

As she walked back home, the cold wind bit at her skin, carrying with it the faint sound of whispers, like ghosts beckoning her into the darkness. The world around her felt more and more like a story, and she was trapped inside it.

The line between fiction and reality had blurred beyond recognition. And Miriam was beginning to wonder if she would ever escape the nightmare she had unknowingly written for herself.

THE AUTHOR'S CURSE

Miriam's anger simmered, frustration building with every dead-end she faced. No matter where she turned, she hit a wall, and the isolation felt suffocating. She had no close friends to confide in, no one to help make sense of the letters or the strange unraveling of her life. The fear was creeping in, if she did nothing, she might lose her sanity, or worse, whoever was sending these letters might be planning to do something much darker.

Determined not to sit idly by, she resolved to turn this ordeal into something tangible. She would write about the letters, documenting every unsettling detail, every shadowy hint she'd gathered so far. This would be her next book, a testament, a warning. If she couldn't save herself, maybe she could protect the village by exposing the truth. Miriam knew the letters would keep coming, but if she never uncovered the person behind them, at least she could say she had tried, that she hadn't given up without a fight.

Chapter 8: The Past Resurfaces

The clock on the kitchen wall tickled relentlessly, each second slipping away into a quiet void. The day had come to an end, but Miriam had barely moved from her spot at the table, her eyes fixed on the stack of old notebooks that lay before her. They had been collecting dust for years, a collection of past ideas, half-formed thoughts, and stories she had abandoned long ago. Now, they seemed to stare back at her like ghosts, silent, accusing, and somehow... alive.

She could still feel the weight of the letters in her hands, the warning from the fourth one still fresh in her mind: *Look closer.* The words had haunted her, gnawing at her thoughts, burrowing into her subconscious. It was as if they were telling her something she already knew but couldn't fully grasp.

As the sun began to set, casting long shadows across the room, Miriam picked up the first notebook, its cover worn and creased from years of neglect. She had written these stories when she first moved to Harbel, a village in this huge plantation that now felt as much a part of her as her own skin. Back then, she had hoped her work would be her escape, her refuge from a world that never quite made sense. But now, as she flipped through the pages, the words felt less like fiction and more like a premonition.

One entry caught her eye, a short story she had written years ago, tucked between the yellowed pages. The title read, The House at the Edge of the village. The name sent a jolt of recognition through her, but she couldn't place why. She hadn't thought about it in years, and yet... the story felt too familiar now, too close to the events unfolding around her.

She read through the notes, her heart sinking with each sentence.

The house at the edge of the village was an imposing, decaying mansion at the edge of the village, its once grand walls now weathered by time and neglect. For decades, the house had stood abandoned, its windows boarded up, its doors locked tight, as if the very air surrounding it had been contaminated with an untold history of tragedy and grief. Whispers of the house's dark past had been passed down through generations, and though many had ventured near, none dared to enter. But one young woman, driven by an unrelenting need to uncover the truth, arrived at the mansion with a heart full of questions and a desire to unearth the secrets that had been buried for so long.

As she wandered through the house's crumbling halls, she felt the weight of its silence press down on her, as though the house itself was watching, waiting for her to uncover what lay hidden. The walls seemed to pulse with a strange energy, and with each creak of the floorboards beneath her feet, she felt the weight of history settle around her like a thick fog. It wasn't just the house that was abandoned—it was the stories, the lives that had been lost within these walls, the lives that no one dared to remember.

ASHA

The first tragedy to befall the house was that of the great man, she had called the character William Doe. William's wife, a young woman who was eight and a half months pregnant when she mysteriously vanished. One day she was there, the next she was gone without a trace. Despite months of frantic searching, there were no answers, no leads, only a growing sense of dread that seemed to hang in the air. Then, by a cruel twist of fate, her body and that of her unborn child were found in the bay, their lifeless forms drifting by chance, a grim reminder of the mystery that had taken her life.

The rumors surrounding her disappearance were many; some whispered that it had been the work of a jealous lover, while others claimed that William himself had a hand in it. It was said that he had been having an affair with the second Mrs. Doe, a striking beauty who had captured his heart. Desperate to rid himself of his first wife and marry the woman he truly desired, William was rumored to have orchestrated the disappearance, removing the obstacle to his new life.

The locals speculated that his dark ambition had led to the tragic end of his first wife, though no one could ever prove it. There were also whispers that the vengeful spirits of the house, ancient and restless, had claimed her as part of their twisted retribution. The truth, like much of the house's history, remained a shadow, never fully seen, only hinted at in the cracks of the walls and the silence that followed.

But that was only the beginning. The second wife of William Doe came with twin girls, bright-eyed and full of life, only to meet a tragic end of their own. Like their predecessor, they were there one moment, then gone the next. Rumors swirled that they had drowned during one particularly violent rainy season, their bodies lost in the floodwaters at the marshy grounds not far from the house. But their bodies were never recovered, and no one knew what had really happened to them. Leah, the second wife, never recovered from the loss. She was left a broken shell of the woman she had once been, her grief so deep it seemed to swallow her whole. The house had taken them all, mother, and children leaving nothing but sorrow in its wake.

And then came the third wife. A few years into her marriage to William, she too disappeared, vanishing without a trace as though the house had claimed her as it had the others. No one ever saw her again, and her absence was another piece of the puzzle that no one could solve. Her disappearance marked the final chapter in the tragedy that had become the Doe legacy.

As Miriam explored the short stories, she felt the weight of these stories pressing in on her, the lives lost lingering in the shadows like restless spirits. The house was not empty, nor abandoned; it was alive with the whispers of betrayal, death, and the sins of a long-forgotten past. And as she delved deeper into the story, Miriam could not help but feel that she was being drawn into something far larger than herself, something that had been waiting for her, or perhaps someone like her, to uncover the truth. She couldn't remember writing this manuscript or what made her write it.

She continued to read, each room in Doe's house held a memory, each shadow whispered a secret that had long been buried. The house was not just a structure; it was a monument to grief, to the forgotten lives that had once lived within its walls. Miriam could almost feel the weight of the tragedy pressing down on her, could almost hear the echoes of the lost souls that still wandered the mansion, trapped by their own untold stories. The Gborie House was more than just a home, it was a tomb, a place where the past refused to die.

Miriam's breath hitched. The Gborie House, it was very similar to Doe's house, its location and structure. She had heard the rumors, the hushed whispers among the village people about the tragic history of the place. But the connection to her story had never seemed significant. It was just a place, an abandoned building that had inspired her, nothing more.

But now, as she reread the words, a sick feeling twisted in her gut. The story wasn't just a product of her imagination, it was a reflection of something deeper, something she hadn't understood back then.

She quickly skimmed through the rest of the notebook, her eyes scanning the words in search of more clues. But it wasn't until she reached the last few pages that she froze. There, written in bold, hurried strokes, was a list of potential story ideas that she had almost forgotten about entirely. Her hand trembled as she read through the lines:

Theft of family heirlooms. Mysterious disappearances. The sudden death of a beloved plantation teacher. Strangers arriving with no past. Secrets buried in the dark.

The words blurred in front of her eyes as the realization hit her like a physical blow. These were more than just ideas. They were predictions; predictions that matched the crimes currently plaguing Harbel.

Her pulse quickened as she flipped to the next page, where a series of notes detailed the village's gradual descent into chaos. She had written about it as a fictionalized version of

Harbel, a small village where the people had become entangled in a web of lies and secrets. She had imagined it then, but now, looking at it, the parallels were impossible to ignore.

The village's façade is crumbling. The truth will come out, piece by piece. They won't be able to stop it. Not the police. Not the Chief. Not anyone. It's too late.

Miriam could feel the walls closing in, a suffocating pressure that seemed to pulse with each passing moment. How had she known? How had she written these things years ago without realizing their implications? There had been no teachers' murders, no missing pets, no burglaries back then. Just stories. But now, they are happening. Right here, right now.

She tried to push the thought from her mind. She had to. She couldn't allow herself to believe that her past work, her fiction had somehow become reality. But the more she thought about it, the more it seemed undeniable. These events had started long before the crimes. Had she somehow written them into existence? Was it possible that the lines between her imagination and reality had blurred so completely that she couldn't tell the difference anymore?

Her phone buzzed again, the sudden sound causing her to jump. She glanced at the screen. Another message from the same unknown number. Her heart pounded in her chest as she opened it:

You're starting to see it now, aren't you, Miriam? The truth always comes out in the end. You wrote it all down, long ago. But it's not just the past that's important. The future, your future is what matters now. And you're not the one in control anymore.

ASHA

The message sent a chill through her, the words colder than ice. She gripped the phone tightly, her mind reeling. It was no longer a warning. It was a threat. A threat that she couldn't escape, no matter how hard she tried.

Her thoughts scattered as she turned back to the notebook. The list of ideas. The story of the Doe's House. The strange, disjointed pieces of her past that had somehow become entangled in the present.

There was something worse, something deeper. She could feel it in her bones. Her fiction wasn't just becoming reality. It was being controlled. Someone, something was using her stories to shape the events of Harbel. And that someone wasn't finished yet.

A knock at the door shattered the silence. Her heart leapt in her chest, and for a moment, she couldn't breathe. She didn't move.

Another knock. Louder this time.

'Miriam?' a voice called from the other side. It was familiar. Too familiar. 'Miriam, I need to talk to you.'

Her pulse raced, her throat tightening as the voice echoed in her mind, growing louder with every passing second. She knew that voice. She had heard it before, years ago, in a place she had long tried to forget.

She couldn't open that door. She couldn't. But she didn't have a choice. Not anymore.

With a shaking hand, she stood up. The room seemed to tilt around her, the walls closing in as the words from the notebook, the letters, and the text messages all bled together. This was no longer just a story. This was her story and someone else was writing it now.

Her fingers touched the doorknob, the metal cold against her skin. And as she turned it, she braced herself for whatever was waiting on the other side..

Her gaze met hers.

Standing there in the doorway was Chitra.

Chapter 9: The Warning from Across the Street

Hen she opened it, there stood Ms. Chitra Shah, the reclusive owner of the small bookstore across the street. Miriam had always been curious about her, a woman who kept to herself, whose store had an almost eerie aura. The creaky floors, the dusty novels stacked high in the attic, the whispered rumors surrounding her... Miriam had always passed by the bookstore, yet rarely ventured inside. Today, however, she stood at her door, an air of urgency about her.

Ms. Shah had come from India decades ago, and though she sold rare herbs and unique books, the villagers seldom visited. Rumors of her being cursed, an outcast from her own family for not adhering to tradition were often whispered. Miriam had heard them, but never paid them much mind. But today, as she looked at the older woman, a strange feeling settled in Miriam's gut. It wasn't just the books or the strange aura of Ms. Shah's presence that gave Miriam pause, it was the intensity of her eyes, as if she knew something Miriam didn't.

'May I come in?' Ms. Shah asked softly, her voice carrying a weight Miriam couldn't ignore.

Though Miriam wasn't one to invite guests into her home, something in her compelled her to step aside and let the older woman in. She couldn't remember the last time someone had visited, let alone someone so clearly out of place in her otherwise solitary life.

As Ms. Shah settled into the worn armchair, Miriam offered her tea, the silence between them palpable. The woman took it, but her hands shook slightly, betraying her calm exterior. Then, with a deep breath, she looked directly at Miriam.

'You need to be careful,' Ms. Shah said, her tone low but firm, 'There's more going on here than you realize.'

Miriam furrowed her brow, not quite understanding. 'What do you mean?' she asked, her voice cautious.

Ms. Shah's voice dropped, her eyes scanning the dimly lit corners of the room, as if something or someone might be hiding in the shadows. 'The things left at your door,' she murmured, her tone cautious, 'I've seen someone dropping them off... more than once. It's hard to tell who they are; the figure is always hooded or cloaked, almost blending into the night. I can't say if it's a man or a woman, but they're careful, meticulous... and they're not stopping anytime soon. From my experience, whoever they are, they're after something and they won't rest until they've got it.'

The unease in Ms. Shah's words seemed to fill the room, and Miriam felt the weight of her warning settle in.

Ms. Shah paused, her eyes flickering as if choosing her next words carefully. 'I don't know exactly what this could be but my guess is that someone is seeking revenge. Someone from the past... something buried deep in this village's history. They think you have the answers, Miriam. They believe you hold the key to their revenge.'

Miriam's heart pounded, the room suddenly too small. 'How could they think that? What answers could I have?'

Ms. Shah raised a hand, silencing her. 'I don't have all the pieces, but I've been here long enough to know that Harbel's secrets run deep. The war that raged for over a decade, the blood that stained the land, it's all connected. And somehow, you could be tied to it. Whether you realize it or not, your past is woven into this town's tragedy. This is not a coincidence.'

Miriam's breath caught in her throat. She had always known that Harbel was haunted by its history, but to hear that her own story might be entwined with its dark past was terrifying. 'What do you want me to do?' she whispered.

Ms. Shah met her gaze, her eyes grave. 'Uncover the truth. Find out what happened. This isn't just some random act. Whoever's behind this is targeting you for a reason, and they won't stop until they get what they want.'

As Ms. Shah turned to leave, her warning still hanging in the air, Miriam was left in stunned silence. Her mind raced as the weight of the conversation settled over her. Could it really be true? Had her own past somehow led her to this point, where she was now a pawn in a dark and twisted game? She hadn't realized how much her move to Harbel had unknowingly tied her to the town's tragic history. But now, with Ms. Shah's warning fresh in her mind, confirmed what Miriam already knew, she was no longer just a writer. She was part of a much darker story, one that might claim her if she didn't uncover the truth in time.

Chapter 10: The Interview

The hum of the studio lights buzzed above Miriam's head, the sharp glow of the artificial lights bouncing off the sleek set. She sat in the plush chair, her hands folded tightly in her lap, trying to steady the erratic pulse that kept thumping in her chest. The air felt thick in the room, almost suffocating, as if the walls were closing in on her. Her mind was a whirl of confusion and dread, a tangled knot of questions and suspicions. Everything she had hoped to escape from had now collided in this small, brightly lit space.

She had never imagined her life would come to this, sitting under the spotlight, about to speak about her books to an audience, but somehow, here she was. A writer, an author, invited to talk about her work. On the outside, it should have been a moment of triumph, a step forward in her career. But the dark twist of fate that had entangled her life with the crimes in Harbel, the letters, and the cryptic warnings from someone she couldn't see... it had stolen the joy from the event.

She could feel the weight of it all pressing down on her, but she shoved it aside, focusing on the task at hand. The anchor, a woman with bright eyes and a professional smile, had already introduced her on-air, and the cameras were rolling now, capturing every word.

ASHA

'Welcome back, we are at Harbel, a small village in one of the biggest plantations in the world. Tonight, we have Miriam Makena with us, the local author whose recent works have captivated readers near and far. Miriam, thank you for joining us,' the anchor said, her voice bright but with a touch of intrigue. Miriam forced a smile, the one she had practiced many times in front of mirrors, but it felt fragile. The woman's tone was light, but Miriam could see the sharpness behind her eyes, the curiosity about what had been going on in the village. She was aware, she had to be.

'Thank you for having me,' Miriam replied, trying to keep her voice steady. She felt like an imposter. What was she even doing here, trying to pretend that her world hadn't turned upside down in the past few weeks?

As the interviewer leaned in, pen poised to jot down notes, Miriam's eyes darted to the darkened corner of the room. The shadows there seemed heavier, almost alive, curling and stretching as if they might suddenly spring forward. A shiver ran down her spine. She quickly looked away, her pulse quickening. Was someone watching? Was it her tormentor hiding in plain sight, listening, waiting? The question nagged at her with an almost unbearable weight.

The fear that had been gnawing at her for weeks now surged to the surface. She clenched her hands beneath the table, willing herself to stay composed. But the familiar hum of anxiety began its slow, relentless rise. Every shadow in the room became a potential threat. Every figure in the gathered crowd felt like a suspect. Could the person sending those letters be here, in this very room, hiding among the faces smiling politely at her?

Her throat tightened as her mind spun. What did they want from her? Why her? The questions swirled, unanswered and haunting. She felt exposed under the bright lights of the interview, like a character in her own suspense novel. This was no longer the controlled world of fiction she had so carefully built, it was chaos, and she was the unwitting protagonist.

The interviewer's next question jolted her back to the moment. 'Your stories often explore themes of fear and resilience. Where do you draw that inspiration from?'

Miriam forced a smile, though it felt more like a grimace. 'From life, I suppose,' she replied, her voice steady despite the trembling she felt inside. 'We all face shadows in one form or another. Writing is my way of confronting them.'

Even as the words left her lips, a cold chill settled over her. Confronting the shadows on paper was one thing. Facing the ones creeping into her reality was something else entirely.

And then, halfway through the interview, as Miriam spoke about her latest work, a figure stepped into view at the edge of the set. Tall, broad-shouldered, wearing a crisp navy-blue suit, his presence immediately cut through the atmosphere in a way Miriam couldn't ignore. The sudden change in energy was palpable, like a switch had been flipped. The air felt colder, more charged.

The anchor turned toward him, her smile now slightly more strained. 'And joining us today is Detective Daniel Jameson, who has been heading the investigation into the recent crimes here in Harbel. Detective, thank you for being here.'

Miriam's breath hitched when she saw him. She'd seen the detective's face on the news several times, and while he was always portrayed with a level of professionalism and authority, his piercing gaze now caught her off guard. He was the kind of man whose presence could fill a room without him saying a word. His dark brown eyes locked onto hers, and she felt an immediate, unsettling connection.

'Thank you for having me,' he said, his voice deep and steady, but there was an undercurrent of something guarded, something that made Miriam uneasy.

The anchor, seemingly eager to steer the conversation forward, began asking questions about the investigation—questions that were clearly scripted and safe. 'Detective Jameson, could you give us an update on the recent events in Harbel? The community has been understandably shaken.'

Jameson shifted slightly, his gaze flicking over to Miriam before he answered. 'We're still piecing together the details, but there's no doubt that these crimes are linked. There's a pattern, and we're doing everything we can to find the person responsible.'

Miriam's pulse quickened. The weight of his words settled in her chest. A pattern. She knew what he was talking about. She had seen it too, she had written it, or rather, it had come to life from the twisted ink of her own imagination. Her books... they were being eerily mirrored by reality. Thefts. Disappearances, Deaths. The events she had once crafted in fictional worlds were now happening in hers.

As the anchor and Jameson continued their back-and-forth, Miriam's thoughts raced. She couldn't shake the feeling that the detective was watching her closely, almost as if he were trying to read her every reaction. And when their eyes met again, she saw something flicker behind his dark gaze. Was it recognition? Caution? Or was it something more? The suspicion she had felt earlier, that this man was somehow involved in all of this, pressed in on her like a vice.

The interview continued, but Miriam's mind drifted. She could hear his voice in the background, steady and calm, but it was as if the words were being spoken through a fog. Her thoughts turned inward, searching for any sign, any hint that might explain why she felt so deeply connected to this investigation, to these crimes.

As the segment came to a close, the anchor turned to Miriam for one final question. 'Before we wrap up, Miriam, you've been living in Harbel for some time now. What's your take on the recent events? How has it affected you, personally?'

The question felt loaded, the weight of it anchoring her in place. She hesitated, her heart thudding in her chest. How could she answer that honestly? How could she admit that her own words, her own stories seemed to have brought these horrors into existence?

'Well,' she said slowly, forcing herself to remain composed, 'it's been... difficult, to say the least. I think we're all trying to make sense of what's happening. But sometimes, it feels as if we're just characters in a story, you know? Like we're being watched from the outside, powerless to change the direction of the plot. It's... unsettling.' She met Detective Jameson's eyes as she spoke, hoping to catch a glimpse of something, some crack in his façade.

Jameson's expression remained unreadable, but the brief flicker of tension in his jaw didn't go unnoticed. He cleared his throat and nodded. 'I understand. And we're doing everything we can to make sure the people of Harbel can feel safe again.'

The anchor nodded in agreement. 'Thank you both for being here today. We'll be following the investigation closely and hoping for answers soon.'

As the cameras clicked off, the buzz of the lights fading into silence, Miriam felt a strange shift in the room. Jameson's eyes were still on her, but now, there was something darker in them. The weight of his gaze pressed against her skin like a phantom hand, and a chill ran down her spine.

She felt it, the danger was closer now, more personal than it had ever been.

As they stood, preparing to leave the set, a gnawing unease settled deep in Miriam's chest. Detective Jameson had been cordial throughout the interview, even professional, but there was something about him that didn't sit right. His manner was calm, almost too calm, as though he were navigating a minefield while ensuring no one saw him flinch.

The way he watched her wasn't the typical scrutiny of an investigator gathering clues; it was deeper, more personal, as if he were seeing something in her that she couldn't. The nagging voice in her mind whispered again, insistent and unsettling: You know him from somewhere. But where? It was maddening, the memory just out of reach, flitting at the edges of her consciousness like a shadow she couldn't pin down.

THE AUTHOR'S CURSE

Jameson's questions during the interview had seemed innocuous at first, but now they echoed in her mind with an almost sinister edge. His phrasing, the specific details he lingered on, it was as if he were more familiar with her life than he had any right to be. Had they met before? Was it possible he wasn't just investigating the letters but somehow tied to them? Or worse, was he writing them?

Miriam's heart thudded heavily in her chest as they walked toward the exit. She stole a glance at him, her curiosity now tangled with suspicion. His face was unreadable, his expression a mask of professionalism. Yet something in his eyes, a flicker too quick to decipher, made her stomach twist.

A thought crept into her mind, dark and insidious: What if Jameson isn't just investigating the crimes? What if he's part of them?

It felt absurd to suspect a detective of such duplicity, but her life was no longer governed by rationality. The lines between truth and fiction had blurred, and her instincts screamed that there was more to Jameson than he was letting on. What role did he play in this story? Was he a savior, or had he inserted himself into her life for a much darker reason?

As they parted ways outside the building, Jameson turned to her with a polite smile. 'Take care, Ms. Hart. I'll be in touch.'

The words were standard, innocuous, but to Miriam, they carried a weight she couldn't shake. Watching him walk away, the voice in her mind whispered once more: You know him. You just don't know how yet.

Miriam stood rooted to the spot, cold dread creeping up her spine. This wasn't just about solving a mystery anymore, it was about surviving one. And somehow, she had the sinking feeling that Detective Jameson was far more entangled in it than he appeared.

She didn't know how yet, but she could feel it deep in her bones. He was connected to all of this. And somehow, she was going to have to find out exactly how.

'Detective,' she called as Jameson turned to leave. Her voice wavered slightly, but she steadied it, locking her gaze on his retreating figure. He stopped mid-step and turned back to face her.

'I think,' she said, choosing her words carefully, 'there's... much we could uncover together. When the time is right.'

Jameson's lips twitched into a faint smile, polite, but devoid of warmth. His eyes, however, betrayed a flicker of something else, something that made Miriam's skin prickle. Recognition? Understanding? It was too brief to decipher fully, but it was there.

'We'll talk, Miriam,' he said softly, his tone weighted with unspoken meaning. 'But for now... tread carefully.'

Miriam's heart thudded as she watched him turn and disappear through the door, leaving her alone outside the building. His response wasn't vague; it was deliberate, calculated, almost as if he'd been waiting for her to say something. Her mind raced, trying to piece together what had just transpired. He had understood her cryptic words too easily, as if they were speaking in a code only they knew. But how? Why?

THE AUTHOR'S CURSE

Miriam leaned against her car, her fingers gripping the handle tightly. This was confirmation, Jameson knew more than he was letting on. Perhaps not about the letters in full, but certainly about something linked to her, to the darkness she was beginning to unravel. The lines between trust and suspicion blurred further, and a single thought gnawed at her mind: This isn't just an investigation for him. He's connected to this, somehow. And now, so am I.

Chapter 11: The Haunting Pattern

Miriam sat at her kitchen table, the flickering candlelight casting long shadows that stretched across the room like dark fingers. The house felt colder now, even though the humidity and heat had been on all day. She could feel it, the subtle shift in the air around her, the unease gnawing at the pit of her stomach. Each creak of the floorboards, each gust of wind, made her flinch. Something was wrong, something deeper than the letters, than the crimes, than the eerie messages.

She glanced down at the stack of papers in front of her, the most recent letter resting on top. The ink was still fresh, the words chilling in their precision, their knowledge. Since coming back from the interview, she had spent hours pouring over every letter she had received, combing through the details, looking for something, anything that could explain how the writer knew so much about her.

But there it was, that undeniable pattern that had emerged. A pattern she couldn't ignore.

Each letter came after a crime, but the strangest part was how the crimes mirrored events from her books, stories she had written in the quiet of her study, stories that had never left her pages until now. It was as if someone had read every one of her books, dissected them, and then turned them into a sick, twisted reality.

THE AUTHOR'S CURSE

The first letter had come after the vandalism in the park, a place she had written about in a story years ago, where a young girl had discovered a hidden treasure buried beneath a centuries-old oak tree. In her story, the treasure was cursed, and anyone who sought it would face tragedy.

The second letter arrived after the peculiar disappearance of a beloved local pet, a cat named Sparkle. Its absence had cast a shadow of sadness over the town, especially for its owner, Mrs. Agnes Worthington. Mrs. Worthington, a widow in her late seventies, had lived alone for decades in a quaint cottage adorned with ivy-covered walls. For her, Sparkle was not just a pet but her closest companion, a source of comfort in her solitude.

Sparkle had been with her for over a decade, a constant presence through quiet mornings and long, lonely nights. The cat's soft purrs filled the emptiness of her home, and its playful antics were often the highlight of her days. To Mrs. Worthington, Sparkle was her family; the last tangible connection to a life once bustling with love and activity.

When the cat went missing, the town felt the weight of her grief. The neighbors noticed Mrs. Worthington sitting by her window for hours, her gaze distant, clutching Sparkle's favorite toy in her trembling hands.

Miriam couldn't ignore the unsettling coincidence. The second letter eerily mirrored a chapter in her book where a woman loses her cherished cat to an inexplicable darkness. In the story, the cat reappeared days later, its lifeless body marked with strange symbols that hinted at an otherworldly torment.

Now, in reality, Sparkle had vanished without a trace. The similarities were too precise to dismiss, and the timing of the letter added a layer of sinister intent. Miriam felt an icy chill creep up her spine.

The thought lingered: Was this just a cruel coincidence, or was someone deliberately recreating the horrors from her stories? And if so, why? As Mrs. Worthington's sorrow deepened, so did Miriam's dread that the letters were pulling not just her but the entire town into a web of fear and darkness.

The most recent letter had come after the death of a beloved local figure, someone Miriam had known since moving to Harbel. A man in his sixties, kind-hearted and loved in the community. In Miriam's book, the death was almost identical: an elderly man, a quiet, gentle soul, who died under mysterious circumstances, his passing linked to an ancient curse buried deep within the village's history.

It was impossible. It couldn't be happening. But the evidence was right there in front of her, too close, too real to ignore. The writer wasn't just a random criminal. They were in her head, manipulating the very fabric of her own imagination, using her words, her books for their dark agenda. For the millionth time, the realization hit her with full force, and she gasped for breath as the room seemed to close in around her. They weren't just watching her every move, they were controlling her story. And that terrified her more than anything.

Whoever this person was, they were no longer just an anonymous figure lurking in the shadows. They were someone who knew her intimately, who knew her thoughts, her fears, her creativity. It wasn't just about the letters anymore. It was about control or revenge like Ms. Shah had said. They had taken her most personal work, her escape, her refuge and twisted it into something grotesque, something horrifying.

Miriam ran a shaky hand through her hair, her thoughts racing. She had always known her writing was powerful, it was what had made her successful, what had given her an outlet for everything she couldn't say in real life. But she had never considered this. Never considered the possibility that her words, her creations, could be used against her. Could be weaponized. Her mind flashed back to the last few weeks, the strange feeling she'd gotten when she first started receiving the letters. The way they seemed to know things about her life, things she hadn't even told anyone. The vague threats that grew more specific with each letter. The cryptic words that taunted her, dared her to try and stop them.

Her eyes darted to the notebook she had kept since childhood, the one filled with half-formed ideas, scraps of stories, and unspoken fears. She hadn't looked at it in years. It was buried in the back of her closet, forgotten until now. But now she felt an overwhelming urge to find it, to see if there was anything in it, anything that could explain why the writer was using her own stories for their chaos.

Miriam stood up abruptly, her chair scraping against the floor, and hurried to her bedroom. Her hands shook as she reached for the closet door, pulling it open with a force that made her chest tighten. She rifled through the boxes of old manuscripts, papers, and forgotten mementos until her fingers finally brushed against the familiar leather cover of the notebook.

It was heavier than she remembered, the weight of her past pressing down on her as she pulled it free. She blew the dust off the cover, hesitating for just a moment before opening it to the first page.

The words on the pages were foreign to her now, almost like they had been written by someone else, someone she didn't recognize. Her handwriting had changed over the years, but this... this felt different. It was like she was reading the work of a stranger.

As she flipped through the pages, the names, the places, the stories, so many of them seemed to blur together. But then she stopped. Her breath hitched, and her fingers trembled as she traced one sentence with her finger. A single line that stood out like a scar. It was from a story she had written years ago; one she hadn't thought about in a long time. The sentence read:

'The writer's words are not just for telling stories, they are the means of creation itself. Every character, every plot, every twist in the story is a thread in the web that can be unraveled, re-woven, or destroyed.'

The words were haunting, especially now. It was as if she had written this message to herself, some subconscious warning she had buried deep within the pages. But what did it mean? Could she have been writing her own fate into existence? Had she somehow, unknowingly, created this nightmare?

Her mind reeled as she flipped through the notebook, her eyes scanning faster now, desperate for something, anything that could explain how the writer was able to predict the crimes, to turn her fiction into horrific reality.

And then she found it.

A passage she didn't recognize, a page she didn't remember writing. It described the recent events; every detail, every crime, each one eerily accurate. The pets that had gone missing. The vandalism. The old man's death. And, most chilling of all, it ended with a sentence that struck her to her core:

'And soon, the writer will become the protagonist of their own story, and the world they created will be theirs to control.'

Her hand flew to her mouth, stifling a gasp. She was no longer just a writer. She was part of the story trapped in it, bound by her own words. The writer was no longer just a shadow in the dark. The writer was her. And she was the one being written into a nightmare.

The silence of the room pressed down on her. She wasn't just being watched anymore. She was being written and whoever was doing it was pulling the strings with every word.

Chapter 12: Unraveling the Connection

Miriam stood in the dim glow of her study, her fingers trembling as they hovered over the pages of her latest manuscript. The room was cluttered with scattered notes, books, and old coffee cups; chaos that mirrored the storm in her mind. She had been here for hours, her eyes scanning the words she had written long ago, as if searching for something she had missed, something that could explain how her fiction had bled into the real world.

Each page, each line, felt like a tether to her unraveling sanity. The crimes, the letters, the eerie pattern was all connected. But how? She had to find the key, the thread that would tie everything together and, hopefully, end this nightmare before it consumed her entirely.

The characters in her books were more than just figments of her imagination. She had always known that her stories were reflections of her experiences, her fears, and her thoughts, but never had she considered that they might be more than that. What if the people in her books were not just characters? What if they were based on real people, people she knew? People from her village?

THE AUTHOR'S CURSE

A cold shiver ran down her spine as the thought settled in her mind. Could it be? Could her stories have been so deeply tied to the fabric of her reality that they were now becoming entangled in a deadly web?

She closed her eyes and tried to think back to the earliest stories she had ever written. The ones she had scribbled in journals as a teenager, the first short stories she'd ever shared with friends. Each one had been born from an observation, a conversation, a fleeting moment in time. The characters had been inspired by the people around her, woven into tales of mystery, heartbreak, and betrayal. But she had never imagined that those same characters could come to life or worse, that they could be used against her.

The sound of a door creaking upstairs snapped her from her thoughts, and she instinctively froze. Her heart thudded painfully against her ribs, a reminder that the house felt like a cage now, every sound magnified, every shadow a potential threat. She exhaled shakily, attempting to steady her breath, and then returned her focus to the manuscript in front of her.

She began reading again, this time with a new purpose. Every sentence, every name, every twist in the plot now felt loaded with significance. She turned to a story she'd written years ago, one about a woman named Helen who had a seemingly perfect life in a sleepy little village until the facade began to crack, revealing her dark past and the secrets she had kept buried. The plot had been loosely based on a woman Miriam had met at a writers' retreat, but the more she read it now, the more it felt like a warning.

Helen had been a character driven by guilt, by a past she couldn't outrun, and as Miriam reread the pages, the parallels between Helen and someone she knew in the village became undeniable.

Patricia Aremu, the librarian. Miriam had never thought much of her when she first moved to Harbel, but over the years, their paths had crossed on occasion. Patricia was a quiet woman, someone who always seemed to be watching from the sidelines, a little too observant, a little too... secretive. She had often offered Miriam odd, cryptic comments about her writing, comments that now made Miriam's skin crawl.

The story of Helen's descent into madness mirrored Patricia's life in so many ways. The betrayal, the lies, the desperate attempt to outrun a past that had been too powerful to escape. Miriam had even based Helen's 'skeleton in the closet' and thinking about it, she had had a rumor about Patricia's estranged brother, a man who had mysteriously disappeared years ago.

The connection hit Miriam like a slap to the face. She quickly flipped through the pages of her manuscript, heart pounding. The more she thought about it, the clearer it became. The characters in her stories were not just inspired by people she knew, they were based on them. Miriam had unknowingly captured pieces of their lives, their darkest secrets, and woven them into her fiction.

The thought was nauseating. Had she been writing these people's destinies without even realizing it? Had the lines between fiction and reality blurred so completely that she had inadvertently written the script for her village's untangling?

Miriam's hands shook as she turned to another story, one about a small-time thief named Frank, a man who lived on the edge of the law and was always one step ahead of the police. In the story, Frank's crimes were carefully calculated, but as the plot progressed, his pride began to overshadow his intellect, leading to his ultimate downfall.

Frank, the name stood out to her. She had based him on a local man, a mechanic named Taji Ali, someone she had spoken to only once or twice when her car had broken down in the village. He had always been friendly enough, but there had been something off about him, a quiet menace in his eyes. She remembered him vividly now, the way he'd looked at her with too much interest during that brief interaction.

The more she read, the more the parallels between Frank in her story and the real Taji Ali became undeniable. The same arrogance, the same reckless disregard for consequences. And then, a chill crept through her as she recalled the most recent crime, another burglary. A safe had been broken into in the middle of the night, its contents stolen, and though Taji Ali hadn't been directly linked to the crime, Miriam's gut told her that he was the one behind it.

As she continued flipping through the pages, Miriam realized that the more recent events, the crimes and the deaths were all unfolding just like the stories she had written. It was as if her characters were being brought to life, their actions dictating the chaos around her. But this wasn't just about her fiction. It was about the people she knew, the people she trusted, who had now become players in a twisted game, where she was no longer in control.

Miriam's thoughts spun wildly as she tried to piece everything together. She needed to confront Patricia, she needed answers. And she needed to confront Taji too. Something dark was happening in Harbel, something tied to her books, and she couldn't ignore it any longer.

But the deeper she went, the more terrified she became. What if she was right? What if the people in her village had become nothing more than characters in a story she had unknowingly written? And what if she couldn't stop the plot from spiraling into something far worse than she had ever imagined?

Miriam slammed the manuscript closed, her breath coming in shallow gasps. The room felt suffocating, the walls pressing in on her from all sides. She had to go to them; Patricia, Taji; she had to confront the people who had somehow become a part of her stories. But a small, haunting thought echoed in her mind: What if they were already coming for her?

She couldn't escape the nagging feeling that, somehow, the lines between her fiction and her reality had crossed in a way she couldn't control. She was no longer the writer. She was part of the story. And she wasn't sure she could write her way out of it.

With one last, terrified glance at her notes, Miriam grabbed her coat and headed for the door, the weight of her actions, of her words too heavy on her shoulders. The village was waiting for her. And so were the characters.

Chapter 13: The Truth Beneath the Surface

Miriam's hands trembled as she walked down the cobblestone path toward the village library, her thoughts spiraling with every step. The early morning fog lingered over Harbel, casting an eerie silence over the streets. She tried to calm her racing heart, but with every echoing footstep, her nerves grew tighter. Today, she would face Patricia Aremu, the quiet, unassuming librarian whose life, Miriam now realized, bore an unsettling resemblance to her character Helen.

The library loomed ahead, its old brick walls lined with ivy and shadowed by towering oaks. Miriam pushed open the heavy door, the familiar scent of books and polished wood filling her senses. She scanned the room until her gaze landed on Patricia, who was shelving books in her usual corner by the mystery section. Patricia looked up, her eyes catching Miriam's in a way that felt both knowing and expectant.

'Miriam,' Patricia greeted her with a small smile, one that didn't quite reach her eyes. 'What brings you in this early?'

Miriam swallowed, feeling a strange tension settle between them. 'Patricia, could we talk? Somewhere private?'

Patricia hesitated, her gaze flickering over Miriam's face before nodding. 'Of course. Follow me.' She led Miriam through a narrow hallway to her small office, where stacks of books and worn leather armchairs crowded the space.

Once seated, Miriam leaned forward, clasping her hands tightly. 'Patricia... I know this might sound strange, but I've noticed there's a connection between the things happening in the village and... my writing.'

Patricia's expression shifted slightly, but she said nothing, urging Miriam to continue.

'The vandalism in the park, the death of Gerald Turner, even the recent burglary, they all match scenes from my stories. And now that I look back, some of my characters bear eerie similarities to people here in Harbel. Like you, for instance. I wrote about a character named Helen!'.....'who hides secrets she can't outrun,' Patricia finished, her tone even. She looked directly at Miriam, her face unreadable. 'I remember that story well, Miriam. It was an inspired piece of writing. Almost too inspired.'

Miriam's breath hitched, the room feeling smaller by the second. 'What do you mean?'

Patricia leaned back in her chair, crossing her arms. 'You may not realize it, but the people of Harbel, the ones who live on the outskirts of your awareness, have always noticed you. Your stories capture more than you know. It's as if you've tapped into the village's buried history, our secrets and you have given them life. We've always wondered if you knew.'

Miriam's mind whirled, piecing together Patricia's words. 'Are you saying... that there's some truth to what I've written? That the events in my stories aren't just coincidences?'

Patricia's gaze held a glimmer of something deeper, an ancient sadness. 'Every place has its shadows, Miriam. Perhaps, unwittingly, you've become the one to uncover ours.'

Miriam felt her pulse quicken. 'And Gerald...?'

'His death may seem as mysterious as you wrote, but that's just it. You're weaving tales that were better left undisturbed.'

The weight of Patricia's words left Miriam feeling hollow, haunted. Her stories had not only touched on truth but seemed to carry consequences. She tried to speak, to respond, but the words faltered in her throat. And then, Patricia reached across the desk, laying a gentle but firm hand over Miriam's.

'There are things about this village, histories and secrets that are best kept in the past. Not everything needs to be written, Miriam. Especially if it risks bringing those shadows back into the light.'

Miriam left the library in a daze, her mind spinning with Patricia's words. Her feet moved on their own, carrying her to Taji Ali's garage. Taji was standing by the open hood of an old truck, his attention fixed on the engine. He looked up as she approached, wiping his hands on a rag.

'Well, if it isn't the village's famous storyteller,' he said, a wary look in his eyes.

Miriam forced herself to remain calm. Taji, I came here to talk. About you, and... the burglary. I think you know what I'm talking about.'

Taji's expression hardened, his face a mask of defensiveness. 'What exactly are you saying, Miriam? That I'm some character in one of your books?'

'In a way, yes,' Miriam replied, the words spilling out before she could stop them. 'I wrote about someone like you years ago. My character was one who pushed his luck one too many times, always playing with fire until he finally got burned.'

Taji's jaw clenched, and for a moment, she saw a flash of something dangerous in his eyes. 'And you think I'm just going to confess? Because you've got some story that matches what happened?'

'No,' Miriam said softly. 'But I think you need to hear this. My stories... they aren't just stories anymore. They're unraveling around us. If you're involved in something, if there's something you haven't told anyone, maybe it's not too late to stop.'

Taji's gaze darkened, and he took a step toward her. 'Look, Miriam, I don't know what game you think you're playing, but you better be careful. You think you know this village, that your stories give you power here? You don't know half of what this place is capable of.'

Miriam's thoughts spiraled as she made her way down the cobblestone path, her footsteps echoing hollowly in the quiet village. The weight of the stranger's cryptic warning clung to her, wrapping around her like a heavy cloak. Moving had seemed like the perfect way to leave her past behind, a fresh start in the quaint village of Harbel, far removed from the chaos of her old life. But now, she wasn't so sure. She glanced nervously over her shoulder, half-expecting to see shadowy figures lurking in the gloom. Are they watching me now? A chill ran down her spine at the thought. The letter writer's ominous presence, the secrets buried within Harbel's idyllic facade, and the unsettling looks she sometimes caught from the villagers; it all formed a tangled web that seemed to tighten around her with every passing day.

Was it even possible to outrun something like this? Miriam's mind raced with questions. If she left Harbel, would the elusive letter writer follow her? Or worse, had she already unwittingly opened a door that couldn't be closed? The realization gripped her with cold certainty: whatever this was, it wasn't bound by geography. It wasn't something she could simply leave behind. As she passed the edge of the village square, her gaze landed on the old church, its steeple silhouetted against the pale moonlight. Even the church, a supposed symbol of sanctuary, now seemed to loom ominously. She hesitated, the weight of her unease growing heavier with every breath.

For the first time since her arrival, she allowed herself to admit that Harbel might have been a mistake. She had traded one uncertainty for another, only this time, it wasn't her past she was running from. It was something far darker, something she had unwittingly awakened. Her steps quickened as a gust of wind rustled the trees, carrying with it whispers that might have been leaves or something else entirely. The air felt charged, like the calm before a storm. As she approached her house, Miriam realized she wasn't just questioning her decision to move to Harbel. She was questioning whether she could ever truly escape the shadows she had stirred.

Chapter 14: A Deadly Game

The sky hung heavy with the promise of rain, a thick, oppressive cloud pressing down on the village of Harbel. Miriam's footsteps echoed in the quiet streets, a rhythm of uncertainty as she made her way toward the coffee shop where she had arranged to meet Detective Jameson. It had been days since her world had started to unravel, and now, with every step, she felt the weight of the investigation pressing in on her like an invisible hand.

Her mind replayed the events of the past few weeks, the letters, the crimes, the way her fiction had blurred into reality. She had hoped that meeting with Jameson would provide some clarity, but the dread that had taken root in her gut hadn't subsided. She couldn't shake the feeling that every move she made, every word she spoke, was being watched. That every step she took was part of someone else's twisted game.

As she reached the door of the coffee shop, her phone buzzed in her pocket. She hesitated, fingers cold as they fumbled to pull it out. The message on the screen made her heart skip a beat:

You're next.

The words seemed to burn themselves into her mind. She looked up, feeling the sudden rush of heat to her cheeks, the unsettling sense that someone was standing too close. But when she scanned the street, there was no one in sight. Only the usual village folk going about their business, oblivious to the nightmare that was playing out in the shadows.

Shaking off the chilling sensation, Miriam stepped into the coffee shop, greeted by the warmth of the familiar smell of espresso and baked goods. But the comforting aroma did little to calm her nerves. She scanned the room and spotted Detective Jameson at a corner table, a cup of coffee in front of him. His eyes flicked up when she entered, and he motioned for her to join him.

She slid into the chair across from him, trying to keep her voice steady as she spoke. 'Detective, what's going on? Have you made any progress?'

Jameson's face was hard to read, the weariness in his eyes betraying the stress of the investigation. He leaned back, fingers tracing the edge of his coffee cup. 'We've made some... disturbing connections, Miriam,' he began, his voice low. 'The recent crimes are all tied to the things in your books. And your name keeps coming up, more and more.'

Miriam's stomach twisted into a knot, her breath catching in her throat. 'What do you mean, 'my name keeps coming up'?' Who is talking and what are they saying?

'The safe that was broken into last night,' he continued, eyes narrowing. 'It was exactly like the crime in your short story, The Last Heist. A safe, a hidden compartment, and the same method of breaking in except, this time, we found something else.' He paused, watching her closely. 'Your fingerprints, Miriam. They were on the broken glass.'

A sharp, cold panic hit her chest. She could feel her pulse thundering in her ears, her hands trembling slightly in her lap. 'What? That... that doesn't make sense. I didn't, I haven't been to that house.'

'You say you haven't,' Jameson said, leaning forward. 'But the evidence doesn't lie. Your fingerprints were found on the scene. And I'm afraid this isn't the first time.' He flipped open a file in front of him, showing her a set of photographs. They were grainy, the images taken from a security camera, but Miriam's heart stopped when she saw them. The blurry figure in the background was someone who looked like her.

'It's happening, Miriam,' Jameson said softly, his voice heavy with concern. 'And it's becoming more than just a pattern. Someone is using your stories to commit these crimes. And you're at the center of it.'

Miriam swallowed hard, trying to keep the panic from taking over. She felt a sudden urge to flee, to run as far from this nightmare as she could. But she couldn't. This was her life now. This was her story and someone was writing it in the most twisted way possible.

'I swear, Detective, I didn't do this,' Miriam's voice cracked, her throat tight with the weight of the accusation. 'I'm being framed. I've been getting these letters, you know. The ones that are connected to the crimes. And I......I don't know what's happening. But this is all too familiar. It's like someone is reading my mind, or worse... they're using my books to commit crimes.' I have been doing my own investigations and so far I have not found exactly who is doing it. My theories so far show that almost everyone in this village is a suspect.

Jameson's gaze softened, but there was a hardness in his eyes. He didn't fully believe her could he? Could anyone? The evidence was mounting against her, and the more she tried to explain herself, the more she felt the walls closing in. 'I need you to stay calm, Miriam,' he said, his tone more measured now. 'I want to believe you, but the facts aren't on your side.'

Miriam closed her eyes, the weight of the situation suffocating her. She had been trying so hard to make sense of everything, to keep the fear at bay, but now it was real. She wasn't just caught in the chaos; she was in the middle of it. And the person who was orchestrating this sick game had her right where they wanted her.

She forced herself to focus. Focus. There had to be a way to stop this, to find the one pulling the strings before it went too far. But what if it already had?

'I need your help,' Miriam said, her voice quieter now, tinged with desperation. 'If someone's using my books to commit these crimes, I need to understand why. Why me? Why these crimes? There has to be a connection.'

Jameson nodded slowly, his brow furrowing. 'We'll dig into it together. But, Miriam, we have to be careful. If this person is close enough to know the details of your books, they're also close enough to strike again.'

Miriam's stomach churned. The dread was back, the fear tightening around her chest like a vice. She felt it again, that sensation of being watched. But it was more than that now. It wasn't just about someone looking at her from the shadows, it was about someone knowing her every move, someone who was always one step ahead.

'You're not alone in this,' Jameson said, his voice softer now. 'But we need to find out who's behind it. And fast.'

As they left the coffee shop, Miriam's mind raced with possibilities. But there was one thought that kept pushing its way to the front of her mind, one that made her blood run cold:

What if the next crime, the next murder was going to be based on one of her books?

And what if she was next?

The game had begun. And now, it was a deadly race to the finish.

Chapter 15: Descent into Paranoia

The village of Harbel had always felt small, the kind of place where time seemed to move at its own leisurely pace. It was the sort of community where everyone knew everyone else, where neighbors exchanged pleasantries over the garden fence, and where the local coffee shop was a hub of chatter, filled with familiar faces and shared laughter. Since moving to Harbel, Miriam had enjoyed and cherished the comfort of this close-knit village, the sense of belonging it offered like a warm, well-worn quilt. Here, she had always found solace in its predictability and the reassuring rhythms of everyday life.

But lately, that same comfort had begun to feel oppressive. The days seemed to bleed into one another in a monotonous haze, and the once-charming familiarity of her surroundings now felt more like an ever-watchful presence. The quiet streets, once a sanctuary of peace, had taken on a sinister edge. Something was different. Conversations had grown shorter, smiles more forced. People who used to linger for a chat at the off license shop now hurried away, avoiding eye contact. Miriam couldn't shake the feeling that behind those drawn curtains and neatly tended gardens, the villagers were hiding something or watching.

The feeling gnawed at her, a constant unease that was hard to ignore. She told herself she was imagining things, but every glance out her window seemed to catch a flicker of movement, a shadow pulling away from a curtain, a figure retreating into the shadows of a porch. The close-knit community that once gave her comfort now felt like a maze of secrets, where everyone kept to themselves, carefully guarded, and perhaps, silently scrutinizing one another. For Miriam, the village that had once been her haven now felt like a trap, its walls closing in with every passing day.

She had stopped leaving the house altogether, her world shrinking to the narrow confines of her living room and kitchen. The once-cozy walls, painted in warm shades of cream and honey, now felt oppressive, as if they were leaning in, inch by inch, with each passing day. The hum of the refrigerator became a haunting presence, a constant reminder of the silence that had taken over her home. Even the sound of the wind rattling the windows—a sound she once found soothing—sent a jolt through her frayed nerves. The lines between reality and the fiction she had woven in her head blurred and twisted. Everything felt wrong, a collection of fragmented truths and lies she couldn't piece together no matter how hard she tried. It was as if the village itself had become a storybook, but one where the pages refused to make sense.

Miriam had always found comfort in writing her book but when life felt uncertain, cooking was the ritual that grounded her. The feel of flour between her fingers as she kneaded dough, the soft puff of a freshly baked loaf of bread rising on the countertop had been her therapy. Her kitchen, once filled with the tantalizing aromas of garlic sautéing in olive oil or the sugary warmth of cinnamon and cloves, now felt like a hollow shell of its former self. Still, she tried to cling to the routine.

Her mornings began with the sharp, familiar hiss of the coffee maker, a sound that momentarily broke the oppressive stillness of the house. As the dark liquid dripped steadily into the pot, its rich aroma curling through the air, Miriam stared at her phone, scrolling absently through the latest headlines. The village, tucked away in a remote corner of the countryside, with vast rubber plantation felt even more isolated these days. Television news, limited to a handful of channels with patchy reception, offered little variety or relevance, and newspapers arrived sporadically, often bearing news that felt weeks old. Her phone was her tenuous link to the outside world, but even that felt more like a window to chaos than a comfort.

She cradled her mug of coffee, the warmth seeping into her hands as she took a tentative sip. It was strong and bitter, the way she liked it, but it did little to dispel the weight in her chest. She told herself she'd make breakfast soon, but she lingered in her chair, staring at the screen as the news stories blurred together, their words melding into a dull hum in her mind.

Eventually, she dragged herself to the kitchen. The silence enveloped her again, broken only by the crack of an egg against the rim of her ceramic bowl. She whisked it mechanically, the pale yellow swirl of a lifeless echo of the vibrant breakfasts she used to create. Miriam had once taken pride in her cooking, in crafting meals that felt like small celebrations of life. Now, the egg sizzled in the pan, forgotten for a moment too long, its edges crisping unevenly. She slid it onto a plate, the act devoid of the satisfaction it used to bring.

Lunchtime offered no more inspiration. She half-heartedly chopped a handful of vegetables, her knife slipping on the cutting board as if even it shared her disinterest. The carrots, cut into uneven chunks, bobbed in the broth she stirred distractedly. They floated like tiny, indifferent islands in a sea that tasted faintly of salt and apathy. She added too much seasoning, then thinned it out with water, though she barely noticed. She sat down with the bowl, spoon in hand, but the soup tasted of nothing.

Miriam went through the motions of feeding herself, but each bite felt more like a chore than nourishment. Food, once a joy, had become another hollow routine, a ritual she performed not because she wanted to, but because she had to. As she cleared the dishes, the faint scent of the coffee she'd brewed that morning still lingered in the air, a bittersweet reminder of how her days had begun to dissolve into one another, each as flavorless and indistinct as the meals she prepared.

Dinner was a somber affair: a single plate set at her scratched wooden table. She made herself a grilled cheese sandwich, the bread browning unevenly on the pan as she stared blankly at the curling edges. The sharp tang of cheddar and the buttery crunch of the toast reminded her, fleetingly, of better days. Yet even this small comfort felt hollow, like she was going through the motions of someone else's life. The food, which once brought her joy, now only served as a reminder of how much she had lost.

THE AUTHOR'S CURSE

Her evenings ended with the same unease, a cup of tea cradled in her hands as she stared out the window, searching for meaning in the darkened streets beyond. The faint warmth of the chamomile would soothe her throat but not her mind, the fragrant steam curling up to vanish into the cold, still air of the room. Cooking had once been her anchor, but now even that ritual felt as fragile as the world around her.

The letters had stopped arriving. Miriam couldn't decide if it was a relief or something far darker. She had a nagging sense that the pause was only temporary, but the silence itself felt heavier, more threatening, than any words the letters might have contained. Each day without an envelope felt like the calm before a storm she couldn't predict. Her phone, once a lifeline to the few friends she still had, now sat lifeless on the counter. The screen remained dark, untouched, the ringer switched off days ago. She told herself it was because she couldn't bear the noise, but deep down, she feared something else entirely, what if someone did reach out? What if they didn't?

Her friends, the ones who used to check in faithfully, seemed to have grown distant. They never directly asked about the letters, as if they instinctively knew that probing would push her further away. Conversations had become shallow, polite exchanges about the weather, the humid days in this village or harmless jokes that avoided the obvious tension. At first, she was grateful for their tact, but now it felt as if they were tiptoeing around her like a fragile vase about to shatter. Were they protecting her or themselves? Miriam couldn't tell anymore.

Sometimes, late at night, she couldn't shake the feeling that one of them might be responsible. Could it be one of her friends who had sent those letters? The thought twisted in her mind like a thorny vine. She replayed every interaction, every word spoken, dissecting their tones and glances for hidden meanings. Was it the friend who had grown uncharacteristically quiet, or the one who seemed overly cheerful, as if compensating for something? Paranoia crept in, infecting her memories and twisting her perceptions until she didn't know who or what to believe.

Her house, once a sanctuary, now felt like a fortress. She paced its narrow halls, torn between the need to keep everyone out and the aching loneliness of their absence. Her isolation had become its own prison, the few unanswered calls and unread text a brick in the walls she was building around herself. She told herself she didn't need anyone, but the echoes of silence pressed down on her like a weight she couldn't lift. How could she trust anyone when even her own mind felt like a traitor?

Her thoughts spiraled. The faces of her friends and the people she had once relied on, began to warp in her mind. Could they be involved? Could they have known something about the crimes? Every word from her neighbors, every kind gesture from anyone, felt like a performance. Was it possible they were hiding something from her? Were they in on this, complicit in the game someone was playing with her life?

She couldn't be sure.

Miriam glanced around the room. The shadows had grown longer, the light of the early evening casting distorted shapes across the furniture. She wiped a trembling hand over her forehead, trying to calm the dizziness that had settled there. It was happening again she could feel the panic clawing its way up her chest, tight and unrelenting. It was as if the air itself was pressing in, suffocating her.

Someone watching, she could not see it but she knew deep in her body that someone was.

Her eyes darted to the window. The street was empty, the silence stretching in every direction. But that didn't mean anything. She had become attuned to every creak of the floorboards, every rustle outside the door. She could almost hear them, the ones who were always watching, always waiting. The shadows on the other side of the glass, the figures that never fully came into focus but lingered just enough to unsettle her.

She had stopped answering the door. No knock, no ring of the bell, no friend or neighbor calling. The thought of opening the door, even just a crack, filled her with dread. What if it was them? What if the next person to step inside was the one behind it all? What if the next letter, the next crime, was going to be a direct attack on her very existence?

The thought gnawed at her, eating away at the last strands of her sanity. She was no longer sure of what was real. Was she truly being watched, or was it her mind twisting the world into a paranoid nightmare? She couldn't tell anymore.

Her phone buzzed, dragging her out of the haze of panic that had begun to settle. Miriam stared at it for a long moment, her heartbeat accelerating with the weight of it. Could it be the person behind the letters? Or was it someone who still cared about her, someone who had no idea the monster she had become? She didn't know anymore. She couldn't afford to know.

With shaking hands, she unlocked the phone, the screen lighting up with a message. She didn't recognize the number, but the message was clear, as chilling as it was simple:

You know who it is, you have always known!

Her breath caught in her throat, and for a moment, the room seemed to tilt beneath her. The floor felt unsteady, as if the ground itself might crumble away at any second. Who was sending this? The sickening thought crept into her mind again. What if they're inside? What if they've always been inside, watching, waiting?

Her gaze shot to the hallway, the narrow corridor that led to the front door. It was empty, but in her mind, she could see the figure standing just beyond the frame, hidden in the shadows. The dread twisted inside her, a feeling of impending doom.

A knock at the door jolted Miriam from her spiral of thoughts. Three sharp, rhythmic taps. She froze, the air in the room thickening around her as her pulse raced. No one had knocked in days. No one came by anymore. Had they ever?

Her eyes darted to the door, then back to the dim, empty room. Had she really heard it? Or was it just another trick of her mind, another fracture in the fragile reality she clung to? She waited, the silence oppressive, her breath hitching in her throat. Another knock. This time, louder, more insistent. The sound echoed through her small home, shattering the quiet. Her skin prickled as a wave of cold dread swept over her.

Her gaze lingered on the door, heart hammering in her chest. How long had she been sitting there, staring? Seconds? Minutes? Time felt meaningless now, her thoughts a swirling fog of doubt and confusion. The phone in her lap slipped from her trembling hands, clattering onto the floor with a sharp thud that made her flinch. She stood abruptly, knees threatening to buckle, her legs unsteady beneath her.

Don't answer it.

The voice in her head hissed with conviction, though whether it was reason or fear speaking, she didn't know. Her bare feet shuffled forward, the sound of her steps swallowed by the suffocating quiet. Her hand trembled as she reached out toward the door, her fingers brushing against the cool metal of the lock.

Another sound. Not a knock this time, but a soft drag, like footsteps shifting across her porch.

Her breath hitched again, her hand hovering over the door handle. Every instinct screamed at her to step back, to retreat to the safety of the house and lock herself away from whoever or whatever was out there. But another thought crept in, nagging and insidious: What if no one is there? What if there never was?

The walls seemed to press closer, her own shadow flickering in the dim light as she stood frozen between action and paralysis. Her fingers curled around the doorknob, cool metal grounding her in the moment. Her grip tightened. This is madness, she thought, but the door opened anyway.

The creak of the hinges cut through the night, loud and unforgiving. She squinted into the darkness beyond, but the porch was empty. The air outside was still, heavy with the faint, earthy scent of damp leaves. The street beyond was deserted, a faint mist curling along the edges of the pavement. Not a soul stirred.

Miriam's chest rose and fell with rapid, shallow breaths, her head spinning. *Did I imagine it?* The question gnawed at her as she stepped outside, her bare toes brushing the cool wood of the porch. She looked to the side, then back into the empty street. There was no one. No shadow, no sign of life. Nothing.

Her hand went to her temple, massaging the dull throb that had begun there. Her gaze lingered on the space where she thought someone might have been standing, and she couldn't shake the feeling of eyes watching her from the shadows.

She stepped back inside, locking the door behind her with trembling fingers. The silence that followed felt deafening, heavy as stone. It was her imagination, it had to be. Yet, as she backed away, her eyes flicking nervously to the darkened windows, she couldn't silence the voice in her mind whispering: *What if it wasn't?*

She sank into the couch, pulling a blanket tightly around her shoulders. The idea that she might be going mad was almost more terrifying than the thought of someone being out there. What was real anymore? The lines had blurred so thoroughly that she didn't know if her fear was baseless or entirely justified.

And yet, in the pit of her stomach, one thought remained, relentless and unshakable: *What if the knock comes again?* And the message on the phone was real, that she could see as she read the message again.

You know who it is, you have always known!

Chapter 16: A Confession in the Dark

The night was heavier than usual, a suffocating blanket that clung to Miriam's every thought. She sat at her kitchen table, the dim light of the lamp casting long shadows against the walls. The letter had come just hours ago, slipped under the door as quietly as a whisper. But its message was far from silent.

The next one will be the hardest. You can't stop it. It's already in motion. Someone close to you will be next. It's your fault for not realizing sooner. The clock is ticking. Prepare yourself.

Miriam's hand trembled as she held the letter, the ink smeared in places from where her fingers had dampened the paper with sweat. The words blurred in front of her eyes, each one cutting deeper than the last. This wasn't a game anymore. This wasn't some twisted fanfic. This was real. And the realization twisted in her stomach like a knife being driven deeper with each breath.

Someone close to you.

The words echoed in her mind, haunting her, clinging to her like a toxic fog. Who? Who could it be? She scanned her mind, running through every name of people in her life, every connection she had, not family as she was not close with anyone, not with her mum or brother, friends, neighbors or acquaintances. But the list felt endless, and yet... too small. The more she thought about it, the more it felt like the whole world was turning against her, closing in on her until there was no one left she could trust.

She had to do something. She couldn't let anyone else get hurt not after what had already happened. But who could she turn to? The police? They'd been no help so far. Detective Jameson had shown up after the first crime, his handsome face serious, his questions sharp, but since then, things had only felt more complicated. There was something in his eyes that unsettled her. Something that shifted, something that spoke of secrets he wasn't sharing. She couldn't shake the feeling that he was hiding something from her. And now, more than ever, she needed to know what that was.

She picked up her phone, the weight of it suddenly feeling heavier than it ever had. She stared at the screen for a long time, debating whether or not to call him. She needed answers, but did she really want to hear what he had to say? What if he knew something more than he was letting on?

With a shaky breath, Miriam dialed his number.

It rang twice before he picked up.

'Detective Jameson,' she said, her voice thick with urgency.

'Miriam,' he answered, his voice low and steady, but there was an edge to it she hadn't heard before. 'What's wrong?'

'I just got another letter,' she said, each word dragging out painfully, 'and it says the next crime will happen soon. And someone close to me will be attacked. I don't know who it is, but I can't....' Her voice faltered, her throat tight as she fought back tears. 'I don't know why they are writing to me.'

There was a long pause on the other end of the line. She could practically hear his mind racing, weighing his options. When he spoke again, his tone was different, softer, more considerate.

'I understand,' he said quietly. 'But you need to be careful. The more you know, the more dangerous it becomes. You've already seen what they're capable of.'

'I can't just sit back and do nothing!' Miriam's voice cracked as she said the words, the desperation finally breaking free. 'I need you to help me, Jameson. I need to know what's going on. I need to know who's behind this.'

Another pause. This time, it wasn't filled with concern or reassurance. It was filled with silence, and it made her skin crawl.

'I'll meet you,' he said after what felt like an eternity. 'Tomorrow. The little Famington restaurant by the corner of Mason Street.'

Her heart skipped a beat, the thought of meeting him again, after everything, made her uneasy. He had always been there, steady and calm, but now something in his demeanor felt off. She couldn't put her finger on it, but there was a distance in his voice that hadn't been there before.

'Thank you,' she said, though a cold pit had settled in her stomach.

After hanging up, Miriam remained seated at the table, staring at the now-empty phone screen, her fingers twitching with the urge to call him back, to demand more answers, to ask the questions she could barely voice in her own head. But she didn't. The uncertainty clawed at her chest, filling her with a sense of helplessness. What had she gotten herself into?

She could feel the weight of the letter on the table in front of her, its words continuing to invade her thoughts. Prepare yourself. How could she prepare for something like this? How could she stop it when she couldn't even stop the letters from coming, let alone the crimes themselves?

A knock at the door suddenly broke the silence, startling her.

She froze.

Who could it be now? Her mind raced. Was it the writer? Was someone already in her house? The panic flooded her, cold and sharp, gripping her chest as if she were suffocating.

The knock came again, louder this time, followed by a low, familiar voice.

'Miriam, it's me.'

Jameson.

Her pulse fluttered in her throat as she stood up, her legs weak, her mind still reeling from the phone call. What was he doing here? Why hadn't he just waited until tomorrow?

With trembling hands, she opened the door, her heart beating in her ears.

Jameson stood there, his face more serious than she had ever seen it. His expression was hard, guarded, his eyes betraying no emotion. He didn't step inside immediately, as if waiting for her permission.

'Jameson what is it?' she asked, her voice barely above a whisper.

'I'm sorry to show up like this,' he said, stepping inside, his eyes scanning the room like he was checking for threats. 'But I couldn't wait until tomorrow. Something's not right. You're not safe.'

She swallowed, her throat dry. 'What do you mean?'

He hesitated for a moment, his jaw tight as he looked around. 'There are things you don't know, Miriam. Things I should have told you sooner.'

Her heart sank. What was he hiding?

'I don't know who's behind this,' he continued, his voice barely a whisper, 'but I know it's getting closer. It's getting dangerous. I've been trying to protect you, trying to keep you safe but it's getting harder to stay one step ahead.'

Miriam's breath caught in her throat. There was something about his words, about his tone that unsettled her more than the letter had. Trying to protect her? But why? Who was he protecting her from, and why hadn't he told her any of this sooner?

'I don't understand,' she said, the fear and confusion leaking into her voice. 'Who are you protecting me from?

Jameson's gaze flickered, and for a moment, there was something in his eyes, a flicker of vulnerability. But it was gone just as quickly, replaced by something darker. 'Because,' he said, taking a step closer to her, his voice almost imperceptible, 'I think it's time you know the truth. I think you've already figured out that there's a connection between you and these crimes, but there's something even deeper than that. Something you're not seeing yet.'

Miriam's pulse quickened. What was he saying? What was he hinting at? What did he know that she didn't?

Before she could ask, the phone rang again, cutting off any further conversation. She glanced at it her breath catching in her throat as she saw the name on the screen.

It was from her brother Andrew.

But what she heard on the other end of the line made her blood run cold.

'Miriam, I know when you came over we didn't get to talk as I was very upset about you never coming back to see me or mum when she was sick. I am still upset but mum told me things about the past. You need to be careful, don't trust anyone including Detective Jameson and with that he hanged up.

Her world, already teetering on the edge of collapse, was about to shatter.

Jameson waited until Miriam put the phone down. Miriam, 'It's about the letters,' he said, glancing over his shoulder, as if he feared someone might overhear. Of course, it was about the letters. It always was. But the tone in his voice, the slight quiver, made her throat tighten.

'I... I can't right now,' she said quickly, her words coming out sharper than intended. 'I have to make a call.'

'Miriam—'

'No, Jameson.' Her hand tightened on the door. 'Not now.'

His mouth opened as if to protest, but her expression must have silenced him. With a reluctant nod, he stepped back. 'You should be careful,' he said before turning and walking away, his figure swallowed by the shadows of the street.

The moment the door clicked shut, she exhaled shakily, her mind already racing. She didn't know her brother at all but she felt like she could trust him and nit was probably time she tried to close the bridge between them after all these years. She picked up the phone and called her brother Andrew back, pressing it to her ear as she paced the living room.

The line clicked, and Andrew answered, sounding irritated. 'Miriam? I do not want to be involved.

I've been getting letters and anonymous messages about the crimes in Harbel. What's chilling is how closely they mirror the stories I've written almost as if someone is bringing my book to life in the worst way imaginable.

The letters had stopped for a while, but now they've started again. And Jameson came by earlier, he seemed like he knew more than he was letting on. He was about to tell me something important when you called. I had to ask him to leave because I needed to talk to you first. I can't do this alone. I need your help.

The silence on the other end stretched uncomfortably long, and Miriam's stomach twisted.

'Andrew?' she pressed.

'Miriam,' he began, sighing heavily. 'I really don't think I should get involved in this.'

'What?' The word came out in a mix of disbelief and desperation. 'Andrew, you're my brother. If you know something, you need to tell me.

'This... this feels like something you need to figure out on your own,' he said carefully, his tone guarded. 'Look, I'll say this: be careful. And maybe... maybe you should look into your past.'

'My past?' she repeated, confusion laced with frustration. 'What does that even mean?'

'I can't explain it for you, Miriam,' he said, his voice firm but distant, like he was trying to put up a wall. 'But you know what I mean. You've always known.'

'I don't know!' she snapped, the phone trembling in her grip. 'I wouldn't be calling you if I knew!'

'I'm sorry,' Andrew said softly. 'I can't help you with this. Just... take care of yourself. And think carefully about everything you've been through. Maybe the answer's there.'

The line went dead before she could protest further. Miriam stood frozen, staring at the phone as if it might bring her answers if she held it tightly enough. Her brother's cryptic words rattled in her head, merging with the lingering unease Jameson had left behind.

What in her past could possibly explain any of this? What had Andrew meant? And why had he chosen to back away?

Miriam sank onto the couch, pulling her knees to her chest as her thoughts spiraled. The sense of betrayal was sharp, but more than that, there was an overwhelming dread. What was she missing? What didn't she know or worse, what had she forgotten?

And through it all, one question loomed larger than any other: why now? Why had the letters, the knocks, and the unease returned after all this time?

Chapter 17: A Neighbor's Secret

Miriam's mind raced as she stepped out of her front door, the cool evening air biting at her skin. It wasn't just the letter that had unsettled her, it was the feeling that something was slipping through her fingers, something she couldn't grasp. The pieces were all there, scattered across her life, but they refused to fit together.

She had started to piece together the patterns, the unsettling echoes from her books that seemed to bleed into reality. But now, the puzzle pieces were beginning to take form, taking on names and faces that were so familiar, they almost seemed unreal. Her own neighbors who were ordinary people, the ones she waved at in passing, the ones whose names she exchanged pleasantries with during neighborhood barbecues that were now at the center of this twisted story. And she couldn't shake the growing suspicion that one of them had more to do with the crimes than they let on.

Her fingers gripped the edge of the door frame as she stepped outside, surveying the street. The small, quiet neighborhood had always been a safe haven for her, a place where she could retreat from the world. But these days and nights, it felt different. The houses all looked the same, tucked behind neat lawns and picket fences, their windows dark as if everyone had retreated into their own shadows.

ASHA

She needed answers. She couldn't trust anyone anymore including the faces she had known for years.

She turned down the street, her footsteps echoing in the silence. Her thoughts bounced between the letters, the crimes, her neighbors, her brother, Detective Jameson. The way the events seemed to mirror the events of her books. It couldn't be a coincidence? She was trying to think logically, but logic had failed her at every turn. These weren't just random acts. They were deliberate. Planned. The more she considered the events, the more she realized that someone in her life had to be behind them. And as she rounded the corner of her street, one house caught her eye: Number 12.

Maggie Thornton. Miriam's neighbor. They had always gotten along well enough, exchanged smiles and brief chats when they saw each other. Maggie had always seemed harmless, a single mother who worked late at the only local restaurant - Farmington. She had a quiet, withdrawn demeanor, a woman who kept to herself but had an air of mystery about her. It was one of those things that Miriam had never paid much attention to, the small details that never seemed to matter before.

But now, Miriam couldn't shake the feeling that Maggie's quiet life was hiding something darker. She knew Maggie had been in this village for years, but what had she been doing before? What was she hiding? Miriam had to find out.

She walked up to Maggie's house, a modest house with a rusty swing hanging from the porch, and knocked softly. After a few moments, the door creaked open, and Maggie appeared, her eyes wide with surprise. Her hair was braided in cornrows and pulled back into a messy ponytail, and she wore a faded sweatshirt that hung loosely on her frame.

'Miriam,' she said, her voice warm but guarded. 'Is everything okay?'

'Hi, Maggie,' Miriam said, trying to sound casual. 'I've been thinking a lot about something, and I was wondering if we could talk for a minute.'

Maggie hesitated for a moment, her gaze flickering down the street, then she stepped aside, letting Miriam into the house. It was quieter inside than Miriam had expected, the walls adorned with framed family photos and faded curtains that hung still in the low light. The scent of stale coffee lingered in the air.

'Sure,' Maggie said, sinking into a couch and motioning for Miriam to sit. 'What's on your mind?'

Miriam's heart pounded, but she forced herself to remain calm. This was just a conversation. She was just talking to a neighbor.

'I've been doing some thinking,' Miriam began, her voice low. 'About the recent events in the village. The crimes. And, well, I've noticed some things that don't quite add up.' She paused, watching Maggie closely. 'I've been reading through some old notes and drafts from my books. And I think... I think someone might be using them as a plan for these crimes.'

Maggie stiffened, her hands folding tightly in her lap. Her lips pressed together in a thin line, her gaze darting nervously to the window before looking back at Miriam.

'What do you mean, using your books?' Maggie asked, her voice tight.

'I'm not sure yet,' Miriam said, 'but there's something strange happening. The crimes, they're like scenes from my stories. They're too similar to be just a coincidence. And I think someone close to me might be involved.' She leaned forward slightly, keeping her voice low. 'I just need to know if there's something I'm missing, something I haven't seen. Do you know anything? Anything about someone's past?

Maggie's eyes widened for a moment, and then she stood up abruptly. The sudden movement caught Miriam off guard.

'Maggie?' Miriam asked, her heart racing. 'What is it?'

But Maggie wasn't looking at her anymore. Her gaze was fixed on the door, her hand resting against the edge of the frame. Miriam felt a cold chill run down her spine.

'I..... Maggie's voice cracked. 'You don't know what you're asking, Miriam. You don't understand.'

'What don't I understand?' Miriam pushed, standing up as well, her pulse quickening. 'What's going on here? Why do I feel everyone keeps saying I don't understand? I know I moved in here and found you a lot here but I thought I am part of Harbel now? What is it that I need to know about this place?

Maggie took a step back, her face pale. 'I never wanted anyone to know,' she whispered, 'but I can't keep pretending anymore.'

She pulled open a drawer in the small table beside the couch and pulled out a tattered folder. The edges were worn, and the paper was yellowed with age. She handed it to Miriam, her eyes full of shame.

Miriam took the folder with shaking hands and opened it. Inside were old, faded newspaper clippings. One headline caught her eye: 'Murder in Maple Creek: Young Girl Found Dead in Abandoned Barn'. The date was over fifteen years ago, years before Maggie had even moved to the village. Miriam's breath caught in her throat as she read through the articles, each one detailing a horrific crime. A girl had been found dead in a barn, her body mutilated beyond recognition. The case had gone cold, and the killer was never found.

But as Miriam read further, her blood ran cold. There, in one of the articles, was a small picture, Maggie, young and smiling, standing with a man in handcuffs. The man was named Samuel Gitau, a name Miriam recognized from the back of her mind. He was a notorious criminal who had disappeared from the village years ago, just after Maggie had moved in. Miriam's mind raced, trying to connect the dots.

'Maggie, what is this?' Miriam asked, her voice barely a whisper.

Maggie's face was stricken with fear. She sat back down, her hands trembling in her lap. 'It's not what you think. Samuel... he wasn't the one who did it. I swear. But after the murder, he came to me, begged me to help him. He said he'd been framed. And I couldn't ignore him. I just couldn't. He was desperate.'

Miriam's chest tightened as the truth began to settle over her like a heavy blanket. 'You helped him?' she asked, her voice catching.

'I didn't mean to,' Maggie whispered. He knew things about me. He said he could make everything go away. But then...' She trailed off, her voice barely audible. 'But then people started disappearing. And things started happening in the village, just like in your books. I didn't realize what was happening until it was too late.'

Miriam felt the ground beneath her shift. This was no longer just a series of mysterious events. This was a web of secrets, lies, and murder that had been buried for years, waiting for the right moment to surface.

And now it was happening again.

'Is he still here?' Miriam asked, her voice barely a breath.

Maggie shook her head, tears brimming in her eyes. 'I don't know where he is. I haven't seen him in years. But... I think he's back. And I think he's using your books to finish what he started.'

She paused, her voice trembling. 'I can't say for sure, it's just a feeling I can't shake. But the thought of it being him... it doesn't fully make sense. He wasn't the type to read books, let alone plan crimes based on them. He never seemed that clever, not in that way. She hesitated, her uncertainty hanging heavy in the air. Still, I can't ignore the possibility.'

Miriam's world tilted again, spinning faster and faster. This Samuel Gitau could have been the person sending the letters but she didn't know him and couldn't think of how she would be connected to him. All she knew was the past was coming for her, and she didn't know if she could stop it.

Miriam's mind churned as she left Maggie's house, the weight of the folder clutched in her hands feeling heavier with every step. The image of the young girl in the newspaper clipping and Maggie's haunted confession gnawed at her. Samuel Gitau was a name she'd barely recognized now loomed in her thoughts, a shadowy figure tied to the horrors of the past and the unraveling nightmare of the present.

But why now? And why her? She replayed Maggie's words over and over: 'I think he's back. And I think he's using your books to finish what he started.' Could it really be him? Or was Maggie just another victim of the paranoia that seemed to infect Harbel like a sickness?

As Miriam walked back to her house, her thoughts began to shift. For weeks, she had been consumed by her own fear, certain that someone was targeting her specifically. But now, another possibility crept into her mind; what if she wasn't the only one receiving the letters? She had never considered the idea before. What if this wasn't just about her? What if the person sending the letters, whoever they were, was exacting revenge on everyone in the village for the secrets they had buried?

Harbel had always seemed idyllic on the surface, but now, Miriam saw it differently. The village wasn't just quiet; it was guarded. The pleasantries exchanged over garden fences and the polite smiles in the market concealed something deeper. Everyone in Harbel had a secret to hide, Maggie had just proved that. And if Maggie had secrets, then so did others.

Could the letters be a form of justice? Or vengeance? Miriam couldn't decide which was worse. She thought of the villagers she knew: Jameson, with his cryptic warnings; the way the baker's wife, Shiru, always seemed to avert her gaze when Miriam walked by; the old couple at the edge of town, whose house had been shuttered for weeks. Were they all hiding something? And if so, what had she done to make her a target?

The folder in her hands felt like Pandora's box, and she dreaded what opening it further might reveal. She stepped inside her house, locking the door behind her and collapsing onto the couch. The silence of the room pressed in on her, the faint hum of the refrigerator the only sound. Her thoughts turned inward. What could I have done? The question was relentless, circling her mind like a vulture.

She thought back to her own past, sifting through memories that now seemed hazy, their edges blurred by time and fear. She had always thought of herself as an outsider in Harbel, a newcomer who had worked hard to fit in. But what if that wasn't how others saw her? What if she had done something, said something, without realizing its impact? What if she was more tied to the village's dark underbelly than she wanted to admit?

Her phone buzzed on the table, jolting her from her thoughts. She picked it up, half-hoping it was Andrew calling back to apologize or offer help. But it wasn't. It was a single text, from an unknown number:

'You can't bury the past forever. They couldn't, and neither can you.'

Her heart pounded as she stared at the words, their meaning clear and ominous. Whoever was behind this wasn't just after the villagers, they were after her, too. But why?

Her mind raced back to Maggie's cryptic confession. Could Samuel Gitau really be behind the letters? And if he was, what did he want from her? Miriam didn't even know the man at least, not that she could remember. But maybe that was the key. Maybe her connection to him wasn't obvious, but buried somewhere deep in her past, waiting to be unearthed.

And if it wasn't him? Another chilling thought surfaced: What if someone else in the village is sending the letters? Someone who knows all the secrets, all the lies, and is using them as a weapon? The idea that one of her neighbors, someone she might pass in the street or wave to from her window could be behind this made her stomach twist.

Miriam realized she couldn't do this alone. If there were others receiving the letters, she needed to find them. She needed to know if they shared her fears, her confusion or if they knew more than they were letting on. But who could she trust? Maggie's words echoed in her mind: 'You don't understand.' Maybe she didn't. But she was determined to find out.

Someone was coming. And Miriam knew, with a sickening certainty, that it was only just beginning.

Chapter 18: Under the Surface

The chill of the evening had settled in, casting long shadows over the quiet street. Miriam stood at the edge of Kimathi driveway, her mind whirling with the revelations of the past few days. Maggie's confession had only deepened the hole she found herself in. Jackton was another piece of the puzzle, a face from her teenage years. Even if they hadn't been close, she'd always trusted him, if only in passing. But now, she couldn't shake the feeling that he knew something she desperately needed to uncover.

She had to confront him.

Jackton Langston had been her neighbor for over a decade. A retired school bus driver, he spent his days tending to his garden, always the friendly older man everyone assumed they knew. Quiet, unassuming, with a kind smile, he'd blended into the neighborhood scenery. But now, she knew better. Someone in her past knew her secrets, and though she couldn't believe it was him, she needed answers about who was haunting her with their knowledge.

With each step toward his house, uncertainty pressed down on her chest. Mirian knew Jackton had moved to Harbel too some years back. Where did he come from, what did he do in the past, did they know each other from somewhere else. She needed to understand his role, if he had one at all.

She knocked, the sound breaking through the stillness and sending a shiver down her spine. Moments passed before Jackton appeared, his graying hair slightly tousled and his usually calm expression replaced with a flicker of something unreadable.

'Miriam,' Jackton said, his voice smooth but tinged with caution. His eyes narrowed slightly, studying her as if trying to gauge her intent. 'What brings you here?'

Miriam took a deep breath, forcing herself to meet his gaze. 'I need to talk to you, Jackton,' she said, her tone steady despite the racing of her heart. 'About the village. The crimes. And the letters. Do you know anything about them? Anything at all?'

Jackton arched an eyebrow, his lips curling into a faint, almost pitying smile. 'Letters? Miriam, I have no idea what you're talking about.'

'Don't lie to me,' she snapped, frustration bubbling to the surface. 'You've been in this village longer than me. You must know about what happened back then. Maybe you've seen things, things people don't want brought up. And now I'm getting letters about it.'

For a moment, something flickered across Jackton's face, a crack in his otherwise calm demeanor. But it was gone just as quickly. He shrugged, his tone distant. 'Miriam, I was just a bus driver. Sure, I saw things. People talk, and sometimes you hear things you wish you hadn't. But letters?' He shook his head, his voice carrying a note of finality. 'No. I don't write letters.'

Miriam's chest tightened. She had come here hoping that Jackton might provide the missing piece of the puzzle. Instead, he stood there, unmoving, his expression bordering on disappointment. 'Then why?' she asked, her voice wavering.

'Why does it feel like you know more than you're saying? You've been in Harbel for years, but where did you come from before that? Do we know each other from somewhere else? Are you the one sending me these letters? And if not, then why me? Why am I the target?'

Jackton sighed, the weight of her words sinking into the space between them. His gaze softened, not with warmth but with pity. 'Miriam,' he said quietly, 'we all have our skeletons. And yours...' He paused, as if choosing his words carefully. 'I've heard whispers about why you moved here. Something you wanted to leave behind. Maybe you got caught up in something bigger than you realized.'

Her stomach churned. 'What are you talking about?' she pressed, her voice trembling.

He stepped closer, lowering his voice. 'I heard you had a connection to a girl named Sarah.'

Miriam's breath hitched, her chest tightening as memories of Sarah flooded her mind. The laughter they'd shared, the promises they'd made and the terrible secret they'd kept. It had been a weight Miriam carried alone ever since Sarah's life was cut tragically short. She thought she had buried it deep, but the mention of her name made it clear that the past wasn't as far away as she'd hoped.

'What about Sarah?' she whispered, her voice barely audible.

Jackton watched her carefully, his expression unreadable. 'People talked, Miriam. They said there was a fire. Sarah and her family died in it. And that somehow... you were involved.'

Her knees felt weak. The words struck her like a physical blow, and she took a step back, her vision blurring as fragments of that night flashed through her mind. The flames. The screams. The crushing weight of guilt.

'I was just a kid,' she said, her voice cracking. 'I didn't know any better. I didn't'

'Maybe not,' Jackton interjected, his tone matter-of-fact but not unkind. 'But someone remembers, Miriam. Someone hasn't forgotten what happened. And whoever's writing those letters... it seems they want you to remember, too.'

'Who is it, then?' she asked, desperation creeping into her voice. 'If it's not you, then who? Who else would know?'

Jackton shook his head, his eyes dark with something she couldn't quite place. 'That's not for me to say,' he replied. 'But whoever it is, they won't let you rest until you face it. You'll have to confront what happened, sooner or later.'

'Confront it?' Miriam echoed bitterly. 'How am I supposed to confront something I've spent years trying to forget?'

Jackton didn't answer right away. Instead, he sighed, his expression weary. 'I can't help you with that, Miriam. I don't know who's behind the letters, but I do know this: Harbel has always been a place where people come to hide. And where secrets don't stay buried for long.'

His words hung in the air, heavy and inescapable. Miriam stared at him, searching for a glimmer of truth in his guarded expression. But Jackton wasn't the one she was looking for. He wasn't the author of the letters; he was just another piece in the tangled web of Harbel's secrets. A shadow of the dark truths she could no longer outrun.

Her chest felt tight as she turned away, unable to look at him any longer. Jackton had confirmed what she feared most: her past was catching up to her, and whoever was behind the letters wasn't going to stop. Not until she faced what she had tried so hard to forget.

As she stepped out into the cold evening air, one thought echoed in her mind: If Jackton wasn't the one writing the letters, then who was? And worse, what were they planning to do next?

The night crept in quietly, casting the trees in shadow as Detective Jameson leaned back in his chair, his office dimly lit by the single desk lamp. His gaze fell onto the cold case files sprawled before him, the papers yellowed with age, words fading, but the secrets they held still potent. Sarah Davies. A name that hadn't left his mind for years.

Everyone in his town believed Sarah had died that night. The fire had ravaged her family's home, leaving only ashes and rumors in its wake. The police report had declared it a tragic accident, an unfortunate outcome of an unexplained blaze that had torn through the house with merciless speed. But while the town had mourned her, and most of its residents had slowly let go, one haunting fact remained: Sarah's body had never been found.

Jameson had returned to his town not only to pursue his career as a detective but to solve this very mystery. As a young boy, he had lived only a few streets away from the Davies, close enough to hear the whispers, to see the looks exchanged among adults who thought children were oblivious. But he knew something wasn't right. Even then, he'd felt an unexplainable pull toward the tragedy, a nagging sense that Sarah's story was far from over.

As he grew older, the questions only grew louder in his mind, refusing to fade with time. How could a fire reduce an entire family's home to rubble and leave no trace of Sarah? Why hadn't the search teams found anything more than the charred remains of her bedroom? And why had the case been closed so swiftly, with so few answers?

The faint creak of footsteps outside his office interrupted his thoughts. Jameson glanced up just as his partner, Detective Laura Moore, entered, raising an eyebrow at the stack of files cluttering his desk.

'Still at it, huh?' Laura asked, her voice laced with curiosity. 'Sarah Davies... Don't tell me this is about that old fire case again?'

Jameson nodded, his expression solemn. 'I can't shake it, Laura. There's something here. I know it.'

Laura gave him a skeptical look, leaning against the doorframe with her arms crossed. 'You realize everyone in your town moved on from that, right? You won't find the answers in this village. You should accept Sarah is gone; It's been nearly two decades. Sometimes you have to let the past stay buried.'

'But Sarah wasn't buried,' Jameson countered, his voice almost a whisper. 'Her body was never found. And I can't accept that we don't know why.' The crimes now and the letters being sent to Miriam who was her best friend? It's connected.

ASHA

LAURA'S EXPRESSION softened, and she sighed, stepping into the office and folding her arms over her chest. 'And you think Miriam knows something about it?'

Jameson hesitated, his thoughts straying to the quiet, enigmatic woman who had unexpectedly become central to his investigation. As a child, he remembered Miriam and Sarah as inseparable, best friends who seemed to share everything. But after the fire, Miriam's family had left town, vanishing from Bassa town and from his life as a young boy.

Miriam had stayed behind, living with his grandmother after her family's departure. When his grandmother passed away, Miriam was placed in foster care, eventually leaving for college. Now returning to Harbel as a detective, Jameson is tasked with unraveling a string of crimes and a chilling murder, a memory stirred. He'd seen Miriam somewhere before, a faint echo of the girl he'd once known. But the woman she had become seemed different, cloaked in a shadow of secrets. Every interaction with her since had only deepened his conviction: she was hiding something.

And then there were the letters she had started receiving, letters that only added to the mystery surrounding her.

'I don't just think it, Laura,' he replied, his tone resolute. 'Miriam was there that night. She was close to Sarah's family. Too close, maybe. And I have this feeling... this sense that she knows more than she's letting on about the current crimes and the letters she has been receiving which are related to the crimes then and now.

Laura studied him for a long moment, her eyes thoughtful. 'Look, maybe Miriam's got secrets, but don't you think you're reaching here? She was a kid too. Whatever happened back then, she's probably just as haunted by it as you are.'

'Maybe,' he conceded, glancing at the stack of old photos. One showed the Davies house in its prime, back when it had been alive with family gatherings and the warmth of home. Another photo, taken after the fire, showed nothing but charred remains and ash, the walls crumbled, every memory erased.

But for all the destruction, there was still one thing missing. Her.

'And maybe not,' he said after a moment, a steely determination in his eyes. 'Maybe she knows exactly what happened to Sarah, and maybe she's been hiding that truth for years.'

Laura sighed, resting a hand on his shoulder. 'Just remember, Jameson, sometimes these things are accidents. And sometimes... they're just tragic mysteries without any resolution.'

Jameson's gaze hardened as he gathered the files and stood, brushing past her on his way out the door. 'Or sometimes they're secrets, buried so deep that no one wants to uncover them.'

As he left, he felt the weight of every unanswered question pressing down on him, but he was more determined than ever. He had no proof, just memories, old suspicions, and an instinct that Sarah's story wasn't over.

And he wouldn't rest until he found the truth.

Chapter 18: The Past

The weight of the discovery settled heavily on Miriam's chest as she stared at the latest letter in her hands. The sharp edges of the paper seemed to dig into her skin, and yet, she couldn't seem to let go. She had read the words over and over, each time finding more layers of meaning, more dread buried beneath the surface.

'You've forgotten so much, haven't you, Miriam? All those memories locked away. But they're mine now. You think I've been pulling from your stories, but you're wrong. I've been pulling from you. From your mind. Your past. The real story. And you'll never escape it.'

Her mind recoiled. This wasn't just some twisted fan drawing inspiration from her books. This was something darker. Something much more personal. They weren't just using her work to recreate the horrors she'd imagined they were using her past. Her own repressed memories. And in the process, they were unraveling her sanity, one page at a time.

She dropped the letter, her hands shaking. The room around her seemed to spin, her thoughts a jumble of panic and disbelief. How? How could anyone know that much about her? About her past?

Was this person someone she knew?

THE AUTHOR'S CURSE

A shiver coursed down her spine as the truth began to take shape, uninvited and unwelcome, in the recesses of her mind. The events of the past few days, the crimes, the letters, her talks with Maggie, the unsettling conversation with Jackton; all swirled together, dredging up memories she had long buried. Jackton had stirred something she had hoped would stay forgotten: the fire.

She couldn't remember what had led to it, but she knew someone else did. Someone who now seemed intent on tormenting her, forcing her to confront a past she could barely piece together. The letters made it clear, this was about the past, and whoever was behind them wanted her to pay for something she couldn't even recall.

Her brother had been far too young when she left, but his cryptic words on the phone about his conversations with their mother before her death hinted that he knew more than he let on. Yet he'd been adamant, he wanted no part of it and refused to help. Miriam had no one else to turn to, no one from that shadowy past she was desperate to avoid revisiting.

And now, another letter had arrived. She stared at it, heart sinking, realizing with a cold certainty that this wasn't going to end. Not until she faced whatever it was that had been chasing her all these years.

Her first instinct was to grab the phone, to call Detective Jameson, and scream into the receiver. But she paused, hesitation creeping in. For the first time, doubt seeped into her mind. His brother had warned her not to trust anyone, not even Jameson. Could he be involved? Could he know more than he had let on?

Jameson had been there every step of the way. He knew about her writing and her books. But now, as she looked back to their first meeting, during the interview when she was introduced as an author, something about him unsettled her. He had watched her too intently, his focus a little too sharp, especially when the conversation turned to her writing. Had he always been there, lurking in the background? Where had he been before the crimes started, and why was he recently asking questions, listening with unnerving precision?

Somewhere deep inside, she knew that Jameson was more than just a detective investigating the crimes. She had seen him before, but the memory eluded her, like a dream slipping through her fingers. Who was he really? Was it possible that he was the one behind the letters? That he was the one pulling her into this nightmarish story?

She shook the thought away. She couldn't believe that. Not yet. Not without proof.

Instead, she went back to the letters. Each one had been a mirror reflecting something from her past, something she had buried deep. The first letter, the one that had appeared after the break-in, had referred to The Gborie house, a place she'd written about in one of her early books, a house built on secrets, on forgotten histories. She remembered the story now, how it had been loosely based on a house in the, a house that had burned down when she was a teenager. She had never told anyone about that fire. No one knew. Only her parents. But somehow, the letter had known.

The second letter had been worse. It described a crime that mirrored a plotline she'd written years ago, about a series of unsolved disappearances in a small village. In the story, the victims were chosen because of their connection to an event that had happened long before, an event that had caused a ripple effect across generations. The letter had hinted at the same thing, suggesting that the crimes weren't random, that they were connected by something that had happened before, something buried in the past.

Miriam closed her eyes, her pulse racing as she sifted through the memories, the fog of time finally lifting as the truth began to break through.

There had been a time, long ago, when things had gone wrong in her life. The night of the fire. The strange disappearances. The things she had told herself she had imagined. The horrors she had long buried. She had been a different person back then, a young girl, naive and full of hope, unaware of the darkness that would soon swallow her world.

It started with a friend. A girl named Sarah. Miriam and Sarah were inseparable, best friends, two halves of a whole. They shared everything: laughter, secrets, dreams. But that summer, everything began to change. Sarah had become distant, her once-bright eyes now clouded with something Miriam couldn't understand. She had always been open, always full of life, but now, she was guarded, withdrawn. And one evening, Sarah pulled Miriam aside, her hands trembling slightly as she took a deep breath.

'Miriam,' Sarah whispered, her voice barely audible, 'there's something I need to tell you. Something that's been not going well with me.' Miriam felt a chill crawl up her spine. Her friend, her closest friend, was scared. But she didn't know what for. She had never seen Sarah like this.

'It's okay, Sarah,' Miriam said, her voice soft. 'You can tell me anything.'

Sarah hesitated, her eyes darting nervously around as if expecting someone to overhear. Finally, she spoke, her voice quivering as she relived the nightmare. 'There's a man... someone I trusted. He...' She swallowed hard, fighting back the tears that had begun to fill her eyes. 'He hurt me, Miriam. He hurt me, and I don't know how to make it stop.'

The world seemed to tilt around Miriam, her heart pounding in her chest. Her friend, her dear, sweet friend was carrying a pain that Miriam couldn't fathom. Her mind screamed for answers, but all she could do was listen. Sarah's voice grew softer, almost drowned out by the weight of her confession. 'He said if I told anyone, it would get worse. He said no one would believe me anyway.' Miriam asked about the man and as soon as the words came out of Sarah's mouth, Miriam's blood ran cold as the full weight of Sarah's words settled over her like a heavy fog. Her mind raced, thoughts spinning out of control, but she didn't know what to say. Didn't know how to fix this.

'I believe you, Sarah,' Miriam whispered, her voice shaking. 'I'll help you. We'll figure this out.'

But Sarah wasn't done. She had one more thing to say, and as she did, her eyes filled with a sadness that cut through Miriam like a knife. 'You can't tell anyone, Miriam. Not yet. Not until we have a plan.' Sarah's voice was firm, desperate. 'Promise me.'

Miriam didn't understand. She didn't know what kind of plan Sarah was talking about, but the desperation in her friend's eyes made it clear. She couldn't betray her trust. She couldn't risk losing Sarah.

'I promise,' Miriam said, though her heart was heavy with the weight of the secret.

That was the night everything changed. After that, Sarah became more withdrawn, more fearful. Miriam could see the shadows growing darker in her friend's eyes, the walls closing in. And as the days went by, Miriam felt a deepening unease, the sense that something terrible was coming, something none of them could escape.

But then, that summer, everything shifted again. Miriam's family packed up and left. They were moving away from the city, away from Sarah. Her father had said it was for the best, that they needed a fresh start, but there was something in his voice, something Miriam couldn't quite place that told her the truth was more complicated. Her father had told her she wasn't coming with them, that she had to stay with her grandmother. 'You need time to think about what you've done,' he had said, but Miriam didn't understand. What had she done?

As her family drove away, leaving her behind with her grandmother, the guilt began to fester. The secret. Sarah's pain. Everything. Miriam couldn't remember why she was left, but she knew it was her fault they were leaving.

And then came the fire.

The flames that tore through Sarah's house that night, Sarah's house, the place where they had laughed and dreamed together, devouring it all. Miriam had been there. She had run. She had left her friend behind.

The guilt she had carried from that moment began to consume her, but it wasn't just the fire that haunted her. It was Sarah's secret. The terrible thing Sarah had shared with her, something Miriam had promised to protect, but now, she was lost. And the truth, the real truth, was more terrifying than anything she could have imagined.

Miriam's heart skipped a beat as she understood. The person sending the letters wasn't just pulling from her books, they were pulling from her life. They knew what she had done, what she had failed to do. They knew the darkest corners of her past. And now, they were using that knowledge to force her into the most horrifying game of all.

The words from the letter echoed in her mind:

'*You think you're the author of this story, Miriam? But you're not. You never were.*'

She had thought she was in control of her narrative. She had thought her past was locked away, buried, forgotten. But now, she understood. It had never been forgotten. And the person who was behind this, the person who was orchestrating this nightmare was someone who knew her better than anyone else. Someone who knew her past. Someone she had failed.

The question now wasn't just who was behind the letters, but who had been watching her all along. And the answer terrifying as it was seemed to lie in the shadows of the past.

The more she thought about it, the more it became clear: the fan, the writer, the manipulator, whoever they were, they were connected to that past. They were connected to Sarah. And they were ready to make her pay for the things she had done, for the choices she had made.

THE AUTHOR'S CURSE

It was no longer just a story. It was her story. And someone else had taken the pen.

Chapter 19: Searching for the Truth

Miriam had thought that leaving the village would bring her peace. She had thought that running away from the letters, from the memories that clawed at the edges of her mind, would offer her the respite she so desperately needed. But as the days dragged on in the quiet isolation of her new apartment, small, cold, and far from the suffocating familiarity of her old life she realized that she had only moved her fear, not escaped it.

The letters hadn't stopped.

They still came, each one more cryptic than the last, each one pulling her deeper into a labyrinth of memories she couldn't afford to confront. Every time she thought she was making sense of the madness, the past seemed to slip further out of reach, like a dream fading upon waking. But it was there, lurking just beneath the surface, taunting her with half-formed recollections of a time she had long since buried.

The latest letter had arrived two days ago.

'You thought you could run, Miriam. But the past is never far behind. The truth is hidden in plain sight, waiting for you to remember. Find it. Before I do.'

She stared at the letter now, her fingers trembling as she traced the inked words. It was as if the writer could feel her fear, her hesitation, their grip tightening with every passing day.

They knew her, knew her better than she knew herself. And she couldn't help but feel that every step she took to distance herself only brought her closer to the truth she feared.

Miriam had left the village, but her mind had stayed. Her past had never really left her, never stopped pursuing her. The fragments of her childhood, the fragments of a broken friendship, of things that had happened before the fire, things she didn't want to acknowledge; they were all coming back. And it was becoming increasingly clear that this was not just a game. This was no longer about someone seeking revenge for the horrors in her books. This was about someone who knew what she had done, what she had buried so deep.

She had to know. She had to uncover the truth, even if it meant facing the darkest corners of her own soul.

The small apartment felt stifling, its walls pressing in on her. She hadn't dared to go back to the town she'd grown up in. The place where the fire had started. The place where everything had begun to unravel. She couldn't go back there, not yet. She couldn't risk it. But her thoughts kept pulling her in that direction, against her will.

There had been a time, before everything turned dark, when the town she was born and grew had been a place of safety, of warmth. But that was before the fire. Before Sarah. Before the loss. And there was something she hadn't seen back then, something that had been right in front of her, hidden in plain sight.

Miriam knew she needed to go back. She had to face it, confront the reality of what had happened and what she had done. There were no more excuses. No more running.

Her instincts screamed at her to stay away, but the letters had made it impossible to ignore any longer. The truth was waiting for her. And it was hidden where it had all started.

She packed a bag, grabbed her car keys, and drove back into the heart of Kakata, the town she had left behind. The streets were eerily quiet as she entered the Kakata, the familiar landmarks flashing by like ghosts of a life she once knew. The old bakery on the corner, the crumbling schoolhouse, the rusty playground where she had once spent endless summers with Sarah, they were all there, but they seemed different now. They seemed haunted.

She passed by her old house, then got to the house that had burned to the ground, the house she stayed in as a teenager when her parents left Kakata taking with it so much of her past and her heart tightened. The charred remains of the foundation were still there, a jagged scar on the landscape. The trees in the front yard, once lush and vibrant, were now twisted, skeletal remnants of what they had once been. Everything was different, and yet everything was the same.

Miriam pulled over a few blocks away from the wreckage and sat there for a long moment, her breath shallow. She wasn't sure why she had come back. But she knew she couldn't leave until she found what she was looking for.

Despite two decades having passed since she'd last stood here, the house was as vivid in Miriam's mind as if she had stepped through its doors yesterday. The pale blue shutters, the ivy creeping along the bricks, the porch where she and Sarah had spent countless afternoons, it was all gone now. The fire had taken everything, leaving nothing but scorched earth and time-worn rubble.

Yet, as Miriam moved carefully through the overgrown bushes, she could still feel the layout of the house beneath her feet. She could picture the hallway, the creaking stairs, the room upstairs where secrets had been whispered and plans had been made. Time hadn't dulled the memories. It had only made them sharper, more haunting.

Her breath caught as her eyes fell on something half-buried beneath a thicket of weeds. The leather cover was weathered and cracked, its edges curling from decades of exposure, but she knew it instantly. A notebook.

Her heart pounded as she knelt and carefully pulled it free, brushing away dirt and leaves. She didn't need to open it to know what it was. She had given it to Sarah, but that summer everything changed.

The memory came rushing back. Miriam had been filled with excitement, her mind brimming with ideas. She had given Sarah the notebook, insisting she write down her thoughts—stories, plans, dreams. 'Keep this safe,' she had said, pressing it into Sarah's hands. 'One day, we'll look back at this and laugh. We'll be famous writers, and this will be where it all began.'

But it hadn't been just ideas and dreams that Sarah wrote in it. Sarah had shared something else, something Miriam hadn't been prepared for.

'Put it in here,' Miriam had told her that day, her tone light but insistent. 'Whatever's bothering you, whatever you're scared to say out loud, just write it down. You'll feel better.'

And Sarah had. She'd taken Miriam's words to heart, using the notebook to confide her darkest secret. A secret that had changed everything. A secret she'd sworn Miriam to protect.

Now, with shaking hands, Miriam opened the notebook. The pages were fragile, the ink faded, but as she flipped through them, memories came flooding back. The first pages were filled with doodles, half-formed ideas, and snippets of stories they'd brainstormed together. But as she turned further, the tone shifted.

Scrawled sentences filled the margins, frantic and raw. Sarah's voice was alive in the pages, her pain bleeding through every word.

'I don't know who else to tell.'

'It's my fault.'

'He said no one would believe me.'

Miriam's stomach churned as the words became more desperate, more fragmented. She could almost hear Sarah's voice as she wrote, feeling the weight of her fear. And then, on one page, underlined and smudged, were the words that stopped Miriam's heart:

'Miriam, you promised not to tell.'

The notebook trembled in her hands as the past slammed into her with brutal force. She had forgotten so much, buried it so deep that it felt like another lifetime. But here it was, staring back at her.

She had given this notebook to Sarah as a gift, a place for her dreams. Instead, it had become a vault for Sarah's pain, her fear, and her truth. And Miriam had failed her. She had failed her friend when she needed her most.

Tears stung her eyes as she clutched the notebook to her chest, the weight of its contents heavier than she could bear. The fire had destroyed the house, but it hadn't destroyed the truth. And now, Miriam was faced with the question she'd spent twenty years avoiding:

The question still in her mind was why had she run away the night of the fire?

Chapter 20: The Face in the Shadows

Miriam's fingers trembled as she flipped through the pile of letters, each one dredging up memories and guilt she'd tried for years to bury. The words on the pages felt invasive, like someone had reached inside her head and twisted her thoughts onto paper. And then, from behind her, she heard a voice.

'Miriam,' Detective Jameson's voice was softer than usual, carrying a weight that made her turn around. He looked at her with something unreadable in his gaze, almost a mix of regret and resignation.

'Jameson,' she managed, tucking the letters away. Her heart raced, her guard up. 'Why are you here?'

He stepped forward, hands in his pockets, his expression pensive. 'Because, Miriam, it's time I came clean. About who I am and why I've really been looking into these crimes... and into you.'

Miriam's throat tightened as she met his gaze, her mind racing. 'Who you are?' she echoed, her voice a mix of skepticism and anger. 'You're a detective. And you think I'm some kind of... criminal.'

'No.' He shook his head slowly, his eyes steady on hers. 'I'm not here as just a detective. This investigation... It's personal, Miriam. It always has been.'

She faltered, confusion clouding her expression. Jameson exhaled, as if shedding a burden, then continued.

'I knew Sarah. Not well,' he added, seeing her surprise. 'But well enough to know that she was... important to someone close to me. And when the fire happened, it changed everything. It haunted me.'

Miriam stared, her mind reeling as the past and present collided in a way she couldn't have foreseen. The words barely escaped her lips, trembling with disbelief. 'How could you have known Sarah?' she whispered.

The man's face was calm, but his silence spoke volumes. And then, like a jolt of lightning, the pieces fell into place.

Her breath hitched. 'Wait... you were that little boy. Daniel. And your father... Jackton.'

The name hung in the air, heavy and undeniable. Miriam's voice faltered as memories stirred, faint but unmistakable. 'You used to play with my brother Andrew and Sarah's brother Alex... back in Kakata?

Her heart pounded as the realization sank in. She could scarcely believe what she was saying. The curious little boy she had once seen running through the dusty streets, laughing with his brother, was now standing before her, no longer a child but a man.

And Jackton? His father? The name sent a chill racing down her spine. She knew she had seen him before, both of them but the connection had been buried deep in the haze of time. Now, the fragments of her memory clawed their way to the surface, refusing to be ignored.

Miriam's knees felt weak as the weight of recognition settled over her. She could feel the past pressing in, demanding answers she wasn't ready to face. 'This... this can't be,' she murmured, her voice barely audible. But even as she spoke, she knew it was true.

'Yes,' he admitted, a sadness creeping into his voice. 'I was just a kid—a kid who heard things he wasn't supposed to, who saw the smoke from his bedroom window that night. My family knew Davies. We all thought Sarah died in that fire. But you know what stuck with me, even back then?' He paused, his voice dropping. 'Her body was never found.'

Miriam's heart pounded painfully as Jameson went on, the sincerity in his eyes making it impossible to look away.

'When I grew up and joined the force, that night stayed with me. I couldn't let go of it. I couldn't shake the feeling that there was more to the story, that someone knew something... and that person might be you, Miriam. I followed your work, read your books, looking for... anything.'

He stepped closer, his voice quiet but insistent. 'But I'm not the one writing those letters. I'm not trying to torment you. I know how it looks, me following you to the village, reading your stories, but the letters... that's not me.'

Miriam felt her breath catch, the pieces coming together in ways she'd resisted. 'Then why didn't you tell me? Why all the secrecy, all the questions?'

'Because I wasn't sure,' he replied, his gaze steady but softening. 'I had to know if you were hiding something... about that night, that killed my friend Alex, their family, about Sarah. I didn't want to drag you into this if I was wrong. And, honestly,' he hesitated, looking down, 'I didn't want to believe you had anything to do with it. But you were Sarah's best friend. I had to know.'

She felt her chest tighten, memories pressing against her from every side, the weight of secrets she'd buried. She couldn't deny that night had changed her life and that she had played a part in keeping it hidden.

'What if I told you,' she began, her voice raw, 'that I wanted to protect my family? My family had just moved and left me with my grandmother a week before. He... he had his own reasons for wanting to leave everything behind, and I...' She trailed off, the memories clawing at her insides. She looked at Jameson, a haunted look in her eyes. 'I thought it was the only way to make things... go away.'

Jameson studied her, understanding dawning in his gaze. 'You didn't start the fire but you know who did. Don't you?'

Miriam swallowed hard, the truth thick and suffocating in the space between them. Her voice trembled as she began, her words weighed down by years of guilt and pain.

'You don't understand, Jameson. No one could.' She drew in a shaky breath, her gaze fixed on the ground as if looking at him would make the confession unbearable.

'Yes, my father came back that night,' she admitted, her voice barely above a whisper. 'I saw him. I saw him start the fire.'

Her throat tightened, but the words kept spilling out, unstoppable now. 'I knew why he did it. He wanted to bury the truth, to make sure it could never come out. Sarah had threatened to report him. He knew she'd told me... about the abuse. He knew I'd be there at her house that night. Burning it meant everything would be gone, Sarah, her family, me... and his secret would die with us.'

She pressed her hands to her face, her breath hitching as the memory clawed its way to the surface. 'But I ran,' she said, her voice cracking. 'I saw him, and I ran. I didn't stop. I didn't look back. I left Sarah... her family... I left them to die in that house.'

Tears streamed down her cheeks as she finally looked up at Jameson, her eyes brimming with anguish. 'I was a coward. I should have stayed. I should have fought for her. But I didn't. I ran, and they paid the price.'

The silence that followed was deafening, the weight of her confession hanging heavy in the air. For the first time in decades, the truth was out, raw and unfiltered, and Miriam wasn't sure she could bear the consequences.

He was silent for a long moment, his expression a mix of pity and determination. 'Maybe I don't understand it fully, but I know enough to see you've carried this alone for far too long. But there's more to this, Miriam, someone else out there knows what happened. They're using your own stories to reach you.'

Miriam's hands clenched, and she met his gaze, the realization settling in. 'You really don't know who it is, do you?'

'No,' he said quietly. 'But I know it's someone who wants to make you pay... or maybe someone who wants the truth to come out. Someone who knows what you did, or at least enough to make you feel they do.'

The truth lay between them, unspoken but understood. For the first time in years, Miriam felt as though she was truly seen, as if someone had peeled back the layers and glimpsed the tangled web of guilt and regret she'd hidden.

'What do we do now?' she asked, the fear and vulnerability clear in her voice.

'We find out who's doing this,' Jameson replied, his voice resolute. 'And we end this for Sarah, Alex my friend and for you. But this time, Miriam, no more hiding.'

She nodded, a glimmer of determination sparking within her. Whatever shadows were left of that night would finally have to face the light. And as much as it terrified her, Miriam knew she couldn't run from it any longer.

Chapter 21: The Final Crime

Miriam sat in the library, her thoughts racing as she sifted through her latest manuscript, trying to make sense of the relentless messages she'd received. The anonymous sender's words had blurred the line between her stories and reality, threatening to unravel the secrets she had buried for so long. It was as if all chapters she had ever written were now being used against her.

As she sat, her phone vibrated on the table, the sudden noise jolting her from her thoughts. She picked it up, feeling a surge of dread when she saw the text. The sender's cryptic words chilled her to the bone:

The final crime is happening right now, Miriam.

She felt her stomach drop. Right now. The final crime. She scanned the library, as if the answer lay hidden in the shadows, but her mind only returned to her writing, to the final story she had penned; a story that seemed more like a warning now than fiction. The story of a fire, the fire that had consumed the life of her character, leaving nothing but ashes and memories in its wake.

Her hands trembled as she typed a reply. What do you mean? The message didn't go. The line was dead. Her heart pounded as fear wrapped itself around her, cold and unrelenting.

She rose, her hands still shaking, and started leaving the library only to come face-to-face with Detective Jameson, his expression grave.

'Miriam,' he said urgently, 'are you all right? Have you been here this whole time?'

'Yes,' she stammered, unable to hide her confusion. 'What's going on?'

Jameson hesitated, his gaze shifting toward the horizon where an orange glow was beginning to bloom against the dark sky. 'Miriam,' he said, his voice a low murmur, 'there's a fire at your house. We got word from your neighbors that they saw flames through your windows. The fire brigade is on their way, but...'

She felt her knees weaken. 'No,' she whispered, her mind struggling to comprehend. She was standing here, safe, but her house was being consumed by flames.

Without another word, she bolted past him and down the street. Jameson followed, calling her name, but her thoughts drowned him out as she ran, her heartbeat loud in her ears. She had written this scene before, created it with her own words, the fire that devoured every last piece of evidence, every last fragment of a haunted past. But this wasn't a story. This was real.

As she reached the end of the block, she saw it, her house, engulfed in flames, the fire roaring as it devoured the walls and roof, licking up the sides with terrifying speed. Neighbors had gathered on the sidewalk, their faces painted in horror and sorrow, but they made way for her, parting to let her approach.

A firefighter stopped her at the edge of the scene, holding her back. 'It's too dangerous,' he said, his tone firm but compassionate. 'We're doing everything we can, but there's little left to save.'

Miriam stared at the inferno, her mind numb. The fire blazed high, crackling with fierce intensity as it consumed her belongings, her memories, her secrets. And she realized then, with sickening clarity, that this was the 'final crime' the message had warned her about.

Jameson stepped up beside her, his expression dark. 'This isn't an accident,' he murmured. 'We've found accelerants around the perimeter. Whoever did this wanted it all gone.'

The full weight of his words settled over her like a shroud. Someone had set her house on fire, with meticulous planning and cruel intent. They had followed her every move, shadowed her every step, and now they had destroyed her home.

'Why?' she whispered, barely able to speak. 'Why would someone do this?'

Jameson placed a hand on her shoulder, a steadying presence amid the chaos. 'We'll find out,' he promised. 'Whoever's behind this has crossed a line, and we won't stop until we uncover the truth.'

She nodded numbly, her gaze still fixed on the flames that had consumed everything she had known. Her stories, her memories, her life, they were all ashes now. And in that moment, Miriam realized that this was no longer just about her past. Someone was determined to keep her silent, to erase her life from existence.

THE AUTHOR'S CURSE

As the flames crackled and roared, Miriam felt a hollow emptiness inside her, a strange detachment that mingled with the rage simmering beneath. She wasn't just a victim in someone else's story. She was the author of her own life, and if this was the beginning of the final chapter, then she would make sure she had the last word.

Chapter 22: This has to be The Final Letter

The letter arrived on brittle, yellowed paper, its texture reminiscent of pages torn from a long-forgotten past. Miriam's hands trembled as she read, each word dragging her back to memories she had desperately tried to bury in the dust of time. She had sought refuge in this apartment, bringing only a few clothes, her most cherished books, and vital notes, an attempt to escape the relentless letters. It was here she had hidden, before everything was consumed by flames. But the sender had found her as soon as she moved in, as she had always feared. There was no running from them.

The letter began with a single, haunting word:

Miriam. 'Tonight. The old mill. Where it all began and ended. Where laughter turned to whispers, and plans became secrets. You know the place. You know me. The final page is ready.'

Her breath caught. There was no name, no signature, just the weight of memories pressing against her chest. Miriam couldn't be certain who had sent it, but the cadence of the words, the echoes of shared moments, hinted at someone she both feared and thought she had left behind.

Miriam felt a shiver run down her spine. The old mill. How many times had she and Sarah spent afternoons there as teenagers, sharing secrets, dreams, and whispers they thought no one would ever hear? The mill had been a sanctuary, their fortress away from prying eyes, a place where friendship had blossomed against the backdrop of its quiet decay.

But tonight, it was something else entirely.

The weight of the letter seemed to press on her, a leaden burden too heavy to ignore. She slipped the letter into her coat pocket, a mixture of dread and strange anticipation building in her chest. She knew she had to go. She knew this was the confrontation she'd been avoiding, the moment that would unlock the truth behind all the horrors.

The drive was grueling, the kind that made every mile feel heavier than the last. The road stretched before her, narrow and unyielding, with the night pressing in close, a suffocating shroud of silence. Trees loomed on either side, their gnarled branches twisting into claw-like shapes that seemed to reach for her car as she passed. The headlights cut through the darkness, but it wasn't enough to banish the memories creeping in from the edges of her mind.

She gripped the steering wheel tighter, her knuckles pale against the dim glow of the dashboard. As the mill drew closer, the memories grew sharper, clearer. She could almost hear the echoes of their laughter from all those years ago, a sound that once filled her with joy but now felt tainted, hollow. For a fleeting moment, she swore she could feel Sarah's presence beside her, light, carefree, the way she had been back then. But the image dissolved as quickly as it appeared, leaving Miriam alone with the weight of what was to come.

Her phone sat on the passenger seat, Detective Jameson's number already pulled up. She had thought of calling him more than once during the drive. His steady voice might have offered some semblance of reassurance, of safety. But what could he really do? This wasn't a matter for law enforcement; it was hers to face. Whatever lay ahead, she knew she had to see it through alone.

The closer she got to the mill, the more vulnerable she felt. Her pulse hammered in her chest, a steady rhythm of fear and determination. The car's heater did little to warm her; the chill in her bones came from something deeper, anticipation, dread, the knowledge that this was the culmination of something she thought she had left behind.

As the dark silhouette of the old mill emerged in the distance, Miriam felt her chest tighten. This was it, the place where laughter had once rung out, where secrets had been whispered in the safety of night. But now, those echoes had twisted into something jagged, and she was walking straight into their razor-sharp edges, alone.

The mill loomed before her, its broken windows gaping like empty eyes, the air around it heavy with the weight of all she had tried to forget. She pushed the door open, the creak slicing through the oppressive silence. Inside, the darkness pressed in, thick with the scent of decay and mildew.

And then, she saw her.

A figure stood at the center of the room, barely visible in the dim light that spilled through the fractured beams. Slowly, almost languidly, the figure turned.

Miriam's breath caught. Her knees threatened to buckle as her eyes adjusted, and the face she hadn't seen in years became unmistakably clear.

'Sarah?' she whispered, her voice cracking under the weight of disbelief.

Sarah smiled, a slow, deliberate curve of her lips that sent a chill racing down Miriam's spine. 'Miriam,' she said softly, her tone almost sing-song. 'You came.'

Miriam swallowed hard, her voice trembling. 'You... you're alive. After everything'

'After the fire?' Sarah interrupted, her voice sharp as broken glass. Her eyes bore into Miriam's, cold and unrelenting. 'You thought I was dead. You wanted me to be dead, didn't you? Just like you wanted to forget what happened that night.'

Miriam's stomach churned. The words lodged in her throat, suffocating her.

'You knew,' Sarah continued, stepping closer, her presence growing larger, more menacing. 'You knew what he did to me. The bruises, the threats. And still, you left me there. You ran, Miriam. You left me to burn while the man who should have protected us turned everything to ash.'

Tears welled in Miriam's eyes. 'I didn't... I didn't know about the fire.....

'Oh, but you did,' Sarah hissed, her voice venomous. 'You saw him. You knew. And instead of fighting, instead of saving me and my family you saved yourself.'

Miriam staggered back, the weight of her guilt crashing over her like a wave. She opened her mouth to speak, but no words came.

'You wrote about it, though,' Sarah said, her tone bitterly amused. 'Turned it all into stories, didn't you? Wove my pain into tales for your readers, twisting the truth just enough to make it palatable. But you can't write your way out of this one, Miriam.'

ASHA

'Sarah,' Miriam pleaded, her voice a desperate whisper. 'I was a child. I didn't know how to stop him. I've lived every day with the guilt of what I did, of what I didn't do.'

Sarah tilted her head, her expression unreadable. 'Good,' she said, her voice soft, almost tender. 'Because that guilt is the only justice I'll ever get. And I intend to make sure it never fades.'

Miriam's breath hitched as Sarah stepped back, her figure retreating into the shadows.

'This isn't over,' Sarah said, her voice echoing eerily in the empty mill. 'I'll be watching. You'll never know when or where, but you'll always feel me. You'll never outrun me, Miriam. Not this time.'

The door creaked open, then slammed shut, leaving Miriam alone in the suffocating darkness.

She stood there, trembling, her mind racing, her heart pounding. Sarah was gone, but the words she left behind lingered like a ghost.

Miriam knew the truth now. This wasn't the final chapter. Sarah had made sure of that. She would always live with the fear, the uncertainty, the knowledge that somewhere out there, Sarah waited for her next move. And when it came, Miriam would pay.

Chapter 23: The Weight of Shadows

Miriam's world became a fragile construct of fear, guilt, and paranoia in the days after the encounter. The memory of Sarah's parting words echoed endlessly in her mind, a haunting refrain that refused to let her rest. She slept with the lights on, her phone by her side, checking every shadow in her apartment as though Sarah might emerge from one.

Unable to shake the suffocating dread, Miriam found herself driving to her mother's house, the place where the roots of her past lay tangled and raw. It was a small, weathered home, untouched by time in a way that made her chest tighten as she stepped inside. The scent of old wood and lavender greeted her, familiar and bittersweet.

Andrew was already there, his concerned gaze meeting hers the moment she walked through the door. She hadn't called ahead, but he had known she would come.

'You saw her,' Andrew said softly, not a question but a statement.

Miriam nodded, her hands trembling as she set her bag down. 'She's alive, Andrew. Sarah's alive, and she knows everything. She reminded me of...' Her voice cracked, the words catching in her throat.

Andrew moved closer, his voice steady and calm. 'What happened, Miriam? What really happened back then?'

She sank into the worn armchair by the fireplace, the memories crashing over her like waves. 'It was my father,' she began, her voice barely above a whisper. 'He wasn't just cruel to me, Andrew. He... he hurt Sarah too. In ways I can't even think about without...' She broke off, her hands clenched tightly in her lap. 'The fire, he started it. I saw him, but I didn't stop him. I couldn't. I was so scared, so frozen, I just ran. I left her there. And now she wants me to pay for what I did or didn't do.'

Andrew sat across from her, his expression a mix of shock and sorrow. 'Miriam, you were a child. You couldn't have stopped him.'

'But I could've done something!' she snapped, guilt and frustration spilling over. 'I could've tried. Instead, I ran, and she was left to fend for herself and her family died.'

The silence between them was heavy, filled with unspoken questions and pain. Finally, Miriam stood, her resolve hardening. 'I need to find them,' she said, more to herself than to Andrew. 'The old photos, journals, letters, anything that can tell me more about what happened. Maybe there's something I missed, some clue about how she survived.'

Andrew followed her as she made her way to the attic, the narrow staircase creaking underfoot. Dust motes danced in the dim light as Miriam pulled open old trunks and boxes, her hands brushing over faded photographs and brittle pages.

There were images of her as a child, her face hesitant and unsure, and then there were ones of Sarah smiling, carefree, before everything had turned dark. Journals filled with her adolescent scrawl lay buried beneath stacks of letters, some written by her, others by Sarah. Each word, each photograph, felt like a shard of glass, cutting into the fragile armor she had built around her memories.

Andrew stayed close, his presence steady and grounding as she sorted through the pieces of her past. 'We'll figure this out,' he said quietly. 'Together.'

Miriam nodded, though the weight in her chest didn't lift. Somewhere in these fragments, she hoped to find answers, something to explain Sarah's survival and her rage. But with every discovery, the guilt and fear only grew stronger, whispering to her that this was just the beginning.

Her guilt gnawed at her, relentless and unforgiving. Sarah was right, she had known, deep down, what her father was capable of. But back then, the fear of him, of what he might do to her if she intervened, had kept her silent. The truth she'd avoided for so long now loomed over her, inescapable.

In the shadows of her grief, Miriam debated her options. She could leave town, try to vanish as she'd done before. But Sarah had found her once and would undoubtedly find her again. And a part of Miriam terrified yet resolute knew that running wouldn't solve anything.

Detective Jameson came to mind more often than she liked to admit. She thought about his sharp instincts, the way he'd helped her once before. But this wasn't a case she could explain without dredging up the darkest parts of her past, without exposing wounds she wasn't ready to show.

Her isolation grew. Friends' calls went unanswered, and deadlines for her next manuscript slipped past unnoticed. Even her apartment felt unsafe, the walls closing in as though they conspired against her.

Then came the next letter.

It was left on her doorstep, neatly folded and tucked into an unmarked envelope. Her breath hitched as she opened it, her trembling hands betraying her fear.

'You still write so beautifully, Miriam. Tell me, do your readers know the truth behind the stories? Or is that our little secret? Don't worry, I won't tell. Yet. But secrets have a way of surfacing when you least expect them, don't they? Sleep well tonight. You'll need your strength.'

Miriam sank to the floor, the letter clutched in her hands. This was her life now, a game of cat and mouse, one where Sarah held all the power and Miriam was left to flounder in the dark.

But even as the terror tightened its grip, a spark of defiance stirred within her. She couldn't undo the past, couldn't bring back the girl she had failed to save. But perhaps, just perhaps, she could find a way to stop this.

As Miriam stared at the letter, a thought began to form, one desperate and dangerous. If Sarah wanted her to remember, to pay, then perhaps the only way to fight back was to uncover the truth Sarah had been hiding all along.

Because the fire wasn't the only secret. There was something else, something buried deeper. And if Miriam could find it, she might be able to turn the game around.

The question was: would she survive long enough to try?

Chapter 24: The Weight of Silence

It was days later when Detective Jameson stood at the door of Miriam's new apartment, his knock barely louder than a whisper against the quiet. He had followed to the mill, watched her retreat into the night, her footsteps heavy with guilt and fear. He had hoped she would reach out, that the night would give her some kind of clarity, but when he checked in on her the next day, there was nothing, no calls, no messages.

The door creaked open, and Miriam stood there, her eyes rimmed with red. Her face was pale, as though the weight of everything she had just lived through had drained her completely.

'Jameson?' Her voice was tentative, unsure, as if she didn't quite know what to expect.

'I wanted to make sure you were all right,' Jameson said, his tone gentle, but there was an edge of concern behind his words. 'We need to talk about what happened last week.'

She stepped back, allowing him inside, her gaze never quite meeting his. The apartment was sparsely empty, almost. The remnants of her old life had been burnt away, and she only had the bare essentials. It was a different life, a new beginning, or so she had hoped. But Jameson could see the cracks beneath the surface.

ASHA

'I'm fine,' Miriam said, her voice distant as she motioned toward the couch. She sat down, folding her hands in her lap, as if trying to keep herself from unraveling. 'I just... I need time.'

Jameson sat across from her, his eyes studying her closely. The last time they had spoken, she had been on edge, but this was different. There was a quiet devastation in her now, a kind of exhaustion that went beyond physical weariness.

He cleared his throat. 'Miriam, I know you're trying to protect yourself, but you're not alone. Sarah... she's out there, and she's been watching you. The night you met her, I heard everything. I followed you to the mill and I know she's still holding onto that pain, that need for revenge.'

Miriam flinched, her gaze shifting away. 'I know. She's been following me, tormenting me. I tried to run, but there's no escaping it. I thought she was dead and I thought I could start fresh, but I can't outrun the past. I left her behind once... and now she's here, reminding me of everything I've done wrong.'

Jameson studied her closely. 'It's not your fault, Miriam. You didn't start the fire. You didn't make your father do what he did. You were a victim too.'

Her lips trembled as she shook her head. 'I wasn't a victim. I... I left her. I ran when Sarah needed me the most. I knew what my father was capable of, and I still chose to save myself. I couldn't save her, and now she wants me to pay for it. She wants revenge, Detective. And I deserve it. I deserve whatever she's planning.'

Jameson's heart tightened at her words, the weight of her guilt pressing on him like a tangible force. He could see how much she blamed herself, how much she had convinced herself that Sarah's anger was justified. But there was more to it than

164

that, more than just revenge. There was a deeper, darker truth about that night, about her family, about the fire that had destroyed a family and so much.

'I get that you feel responsible, but this isn't just about you, Miriam,' he said softly. 'It's about what happened to Sarah, to your family, to the town of Kakata. You've both been living with this for too long, and it's eating away at you. But you're not the only one who needs to be held accountable.'

Miriam's eyes flickered with a mixture of confusion and pain. 'What do you mean?'

Jameson's gaze hardened, the detective in him taking over as he leaned forward. 'Miriam, your father, he's dead. We both know that. But there's something else we need to uncover. Sarah may want revenge, but there are others who still need answers. People in Kakata deserve to know what really happened that night. The truth about your father... about the fire.'

Miriam's voice trembled. 'But he's gone, Detective. My father is dead. He was the one who did this. He's the one who caused everything.'

'I know,' Jameson replied, his voice firm. 'But there's more to the story than that. There's more to Sarah's rage than just the fire, and it's tied to everything that happened before. I need to find the truth, Miriam. Not just for Sarah, but for Kakata, for everyone who's been living with the consequences of that night.'

Miriam's hands clenched into fists at her sides. 'What does it matter? No one can bring back what's been lost. My father is gone. Sarah...' She choked on her words, the emotions finally breaking through the cracks. 'Sarah is right. She has every right to hate me. I left her behind, and I've never been able to forgive myself for it.'

Jameson sat there, watching her unravel before him. He wanted to tell her that she wasn't alone, that she didn't have to carry this weight by herself. But the truth was, he didn't know how to fix this. He didn't know how to make her see that the past wasn't her fault, that she wasn't responsible for everything that had happened to Sarah.

'I know it's hard,' he said, his voice quiet. 'But we can't let Sarah continue to control this. We can't let her think she's the only one who matters in this. There are people out there who need justice too.' And I need to know if she is responsible for the crimes in Harbel, the murder too of Gerald Turner.

Miriam looked up at him, her expression raw with vulnerability. 'And what about me, Detective? What do I get out of this? How do I make up for the things I've done?'

Jameson stood, his jaw tight as he looked down at her. 'I can't answer that for you. But what I can tell you is that Sarah's not the only one who deserves justice. You need to find a way to make peace with what happened. You can't keep running from it, Miriam. Not anymore.'

He turned to leave, his footsteps heavy in the silence that followed him. But before he reached the door, he stopped and glanced back at her.

'I'll keep investigating, Miriam. I'll find Sarah, but I won't stop until the full truth is out there. The fire, the pain, the lies... they need to be faced. But this fight,' he said, his voice hardening, 'it's not just about justice anymore. It's about you keeping your sanity through it all.'

Miriam stayed where she was, her body slumped with the weight of the truth she had never wanted to face. She couldn't undo the past. She couldn't make it right. And now, with Sarah out there somewhere, waiting for her to pay, she wasn't sure how much longer she could keep going.

But Jameson was right. The fight for justice was far from over. And it wasn't just about finding Sarah anymore. It was about finding a way to live with what had happened and facing the ghosts that would haunt her for the rest of her life.

Also by Asha

The Realm of Echoing Hearts: Adventures Beyond the Veil
The Author's Curse
365 Days of Positivity Quotes